Journey *with* Zeke

Gift or Curse

LYNETTE TEACHOUT

BALBOA
PRESS
A DIVISION OF HAY HOUSE

Copyright © 2012 by Lynette Teachout.

All rights reserved. No part of this book may be used or reproduced by any means, graphic, electronic, or mechanical, including photocopying, recording, taping or by any information storage retrieval system without the written permission of the publisher except in the case of brief quotations embodied in critical articles and reviews.

ISBN: 978-1-4525-5533-1 (sc)
ISBN: 978-1-4525-5534-8 (e)
ISBN: 978-1-4525-5535-5 (hc)

Library of Congress Control Number: 2012913098

Balboa Press books may be ordered through booksellers or by contacting:

Balboa Press
A Division of Hay House
1663 Liberty Drive
Bloomington, IN 47403
www.balboapress.com
1-(877) 407-4847

Because of the dynamic nature of the Internet, any web addresses or links contained in this book may have changed since publication and may no longer be valid. The views expressed in this work are solely those of the author and do not necessarily reflect the views of the publisher, and the publisher hereby disclaims any responsibility for them.

The author of this book does not dispense medical advice or prescribe the use of any technique as a form of treatment for physical, emotional, or medical problems without the advice of a physician, either directly or indirectly. The intent of the author is only to offer information of a general nature to help you in your quest for emotional and spiritual well-being. In the event you use any of the information in this book for yourself, which is your constitutional right, the author and the publisher assume no responsibility for your actions.

Any people depicted in stock imagery provided by Thinkstock are models, and such images are being used for illustrative purposes only.
Certain stock imagery © Thinkstock.

Printed in the United States of America

Balboa Press rev. date: 09/17/12

"We are all on a

        Spiritual journey…

                Gift or Curse…

                      The choice is yours."

Dedicated to:

All that dream!

Chapter 1

STANDING BEFORE ZEKE WAS AN Indian lady. As in the other dreams, she was wearing a long tan dress with black beading on the front, a thin piece of material belting it at the waist. A beaded headband sat on her head, decorating her long dark hair. The head band had a single feather that rose above the back of her head. What was odd about her was that she appeared to be floating. Even stranger was that he had seen her several times now, but she never spoke. He thought that she was kind, intelligent and very giving. Giving of what, he didn't know; it was just something that he sensed.

This time, as a few times before, a beautiful white wolf was sitting at her side. He knew there was a special purpose to her being there, and to the fact that a white wolf was with her now, although he didn't fully understand what the purpose could be. He asked the Indian lady about the white wolf, thinking that maybe this time she might talk to him, but she didn't answer. Then, just like all the other times, they both just faded away.

"What time is it?" thought Zeke, as he struggled to waken. Glancing over at his alarm clock he saw that it was 8:30 a.m. Slowly, he stretched his arms above his head as he thought about the dream he had just had and wondered again why he was having these dreams. He knew he should get up and get around. It was Saturday and there was always so much to do. Instead of getting up he continued to lie in bed. He could hear the birds chirping outside his window as he once again yawned. He turned to face his bedroom window, as he decided fifteen more minutes and then he would get up.

Zeke loved Saturdays. It was hard to believe that a week had already gone by. It was just last Saturday that he had turned thirteen. They had celebrated with a big party and he had received some really cool gifts. One of the best gifts was the X-Box game from his friend Justin. They had an ongoing competition about who was best at the game. The last time the two had played against each other Justin had won. Zeke was determined not to let that happen again. He practiced all week after school and felt confident that he would whip Justin the next time they played. Smiling to himself, he suddenly knew exactly what he was going to do today. He would call Justin and invite him over to play. He would show his friend that he was in fact the true champion.

As Zeke continued to lie in bed imagining the surprised look on his friend's face when he beat him, he heard a familiar voice calling his name. He hollered back, "Yeah, Dad?" Zeke knew from the sound of footsteps that his dad was coming to his room. He quickly sat up and watched as his bedroom door opened.

"You going with us today, Buddy?" asked Dad.

"Going where?"

"Well, the last I remember, you were going to go camping with your brother and me."

Suddenly wide awake, Zeke responded, "Oh yeah, Dad. I'm coming! I totally forgot. Don't leave without me!"

"Then you'd better get up and get dressed. We're leaving within the hour." As Dad shut his bedroom door, Zeke jumped out of bed and ran to his closet. He wondered how he could have forgotten about the camping trip. He always looked forward to the fresh smell of pine, swimming, eating marshmallows, and sitting around the campfire after dark listening to his brother's scary ghost stories.

Downstairs, Griffen, two years older than Zeke, was eating breakfast. He, too, was excited about going camping. He loved swimming, fishing and scaring the pants off of his little brother with his ghost stories. His dad grabbed a bowl from the cupboard and joined him at the table. Griffen passed him the box of cereal and milk.

"Did you wake him up, Dad?"

"Yes, Zeke's up. I thought he'd be the first one down here this morning after all his excitement about going." Dad enjoyed camping with his sons, as it was a family tradition from his youth. Wanting to make sure his city boys were well acquainted with nature's beauty and mystery, he planned as many camping trips or nature hikes as he possibly could.

Griffen, who had become a great lover of nature, nodded in agreement. "All I heard about yesterday from Zeke was camping-this and fishing-that. He wouldn't quit!" They both laughed.

"By the way, Griffen, I would appreciate it if you would not tell your ghost stories this time." Dad peered over the cereal box to judge his son's reaction.

"Oh, come on, Dad, I love those stories. Not telling them takes away all the fun," whined Griffen.

"I know, son, but Zeke's been obsessing over his strange dreams about some Indian lady and a white wolf. I don't think it's a good idea."

"I know, Dad, but they're just dreams! I don't think a dream is going to hurt you, is it?"

"No, son, it isn't, but I still don't want you scaring your brother with your stories."

Sighing, Griffen replied, "Okay, Dad."

In the background they could hear Zeke running down the stairs to join them for breakfast. In a flash, Zeke ran across the kitchen, opened the cupboard, and grabbed a bowl. He grabbed the cereal and sat down in a chair. "Okay, Dad, I'm all packed and ready to go! When we get there can I go swimming right away?"

"We have to set up the camp and gather some wood first," answered Dad, who was a firm believer that you needed to teach your children that life was not all fun and games; instead, fun was a reward after the work had been done.

"Okay," said Zeke, as he shoved more cereal into his already full mouth. He was accustomed to the camping routine and knew from experience that setting up camp and gathering the wood would not take all that long. There would be plenty of time for swimming.

Having finished his bowl of cereal, Griffen took it to the sink and then looked at his dad. "I'm going to make sure the fishing poles are in the truck."

"I'll go with you," replied Dad.

Grabbing his bowl, Dad headed for the sink and looked back at Zeke. Before his dad could say a word, he blurted, "I know, Dad. I'll take care of my bowl." Dad nodded and headed to the garage.

In the garage, Griffen double-checked the truck. Dad had packed the truck the night before with camping and fishing gear, but Griffen wanted to take a look to make sure he had not forgotten anything. "Hey, Dad, it looks like everything is packed. So whenever Zekey Boy is ready, I'm ready."

"Thank you, Griffen," answered Dad. At that exact moment the garage door flew open and Zeke charged out excitedly. "Let's go!"

Griffen loved his brother unconditionally, but there were many times that he found him to be totally annoying. This was one of those times. Zeke always seemed to want the spotlight. Griffen rolled his eyes in Zeke's direction. Zeke noticed the eye roll and made a face back at him. Griffen retaliated, "Dad, can we leave him home, please?"

"Don't be funny, Griffen," replied Dad, while giving him a "you know better" look. Dad knew that the brothers would quickly escalate their squabbling if he didn't quickly change the subject. He returned his attention to his youngest son. "Did you say good-bye to Mom?"

"Yep," responded Zeke, "and I gave her a hug. It's cool."

"Okay, then. Let's double-check our list to make sure we didn't forget anything. Tent?"

Both boys responded, "Yep."

"Sleeping bags?"

"Yep."

"Fishing poles?"

"Yep."

"Flashlights?"

"Yep."

"Cooler?"

"Yep."

The list continued until everything that they needed for the camping trip was accounted for. With the list checked and double checked, Dad folded the piece of paper and put it in his pocket. "Let's get going," he announced, as he closed the tailgate.

"I call shot gun!" yelled Zeke.

"No way," countered Griffen. "It's my turn to sit in the front seat." The brothers looked at their dad and waited for him to decide.

Dad shook his head from side to side. Smiling, he asked his sons to pick a number between one and ten. It was an old fashioned way of not showing either son favoritism. The boys understood the rules well.

Zeke, wanting to be the first, quickly responded, "Eight!" Griffen followed with the number three.

"The number was seven," announced Dad. "It appears that Zeke will be sitting in the front seat this time. Griffen, you will get the front on the way back home." While the boys were getting situated in the truck, Dad went back into the house to let Mom know they were leaving. Ten minutes later they pulled out of the driveway on their way to Mystic Lake. As they drove, they teased each other about which one of them would catch the biggest fish. Time flew by and before they knew it, they had arrived.

After scouting for just the right campsite, Dad parked the truck. He was an expert at camping and knew the importance of making sure you were on high ground in case it rained. That day there was no rain in the forecast, but one never knew when a thunderstorm might pop up. He also wanted to set up camp close to the lake. Later, they would unload the boat and leave it in the water overnight. They were camping in a pretty isolated location, however there could be other campers in the area. He didn't want someone messing around with the boat or taking it for a joy ride.

Everyone piled out of the car and started unloading the camping gear. Within minutes Dad and the brothers had their tents set up. They knew that when these chores were done the real fun would begin.

"Okay, Dad, we're leaving to find some firewood," announced Griffen.

"Don't go far, you two. Just scout around here. We have some fishing to do, plus, Zeke wants to go swimming."

Griffen smiled as he replied, "Okay." He knew that Dad was a man of his word. When he said they were going to do something, they did.

The brothers took off running. "Let's take this trail!" exclaimed Zeke, as he entered the woods. It was a narrow trail that had thick brush on each side of the path, leaving Griffen no choice but to follow. Knowing that he was a much faster runner than his younger brother, Griffen felt irritated as he had to keep pace behind his slower brother. He would let it go for now, but as soon as the path widened he would take the lead.

The brothers loved the woods. They enjoyed the fresh smell of the pine trees, listening to the birds, and the excitement of discovery. It was as if the woods were filled with mystery and magic. You never knew what you were going to find or what you were going to see.

Running at a good pace, Zeke led the way as the brothers moved freely through the woods. Griffen was right on his heels, pushing him all the way to run faster. Rounding a bend, Zeke came to a sudden stop, making Griffen stumble into him. Reflexes took over as Griffen reached out to keep his younger brother from falling. His quick action kept both of them from landing on the ground. Griffen was about to let loose with some choice words when he noticed that Zeke had a funny look on his face and was pointing at something. He turned to see what it was.

"Wow!" said Zeke, "I wasn't expecting to find a cemetery."

"Me neither," answered Griffen, with a puzzled look on his face. They had camped many times at Mystic Lake, and never before had they come across this cemetery.

"Let's go check it out," encouraged Zeke.

"No, we don't have time right now," answered Griffen. "Dad wants to go fishing and we need to get the firewood." Noticing Zeke's look of disappointment, Griffen quickly added, "Tell you what, we'll come back later tonight and visit the cemetery after Dad has gone to bed." He didn't mention the fact that he was filled with curiosity about the cemetery. Dad had insisted that he could not tell any ghost stories, but he hadn't mentioned anything about not going to a cemetery. That would surely freak Zeke out, maybe even more than a ghost story! He chuckled to himself as he visualized his brother screaming.

Zeke stood there for a moment looking at his brother. Griffen could tell that he was considering the offer. The cemetery looked pretty spooky, and as much as Zeke loved ghost stories, he was a chicken when it came right down to it. Not wanting to miss the opportunity to scare his younger brother, Griffen decided to egg him on, "Oh, come on, Zeke, don't be such a scaredy-cat."

"I'm not scared," retorted Zeke.

"Fine," said Griffen, "Prove it!"

There was something about the cemetery that Zeke couldn't quite put his finger on. It had a peculiar air about it, and he was very anxious to explore it. But as spooky as it looked during the daylight hours, he could only imagine how unnerving it would be after dark. He really did want to come back and take a look around, but he wasn't sure if he wanted to do it at night. "I'll come if Dad comes, too."

Griffen's response was firm. "No, do not speak a word of our plan to Dad. We are doing this by ourselves."

"Why can't Dad come with us?" questioned Zeke. It would seem safer if Dad was along.

"Just because, that's why," responded Griffen. He knew that their dad would never approve of them visiting a cemetery after dark. "If you want to come with me tonight, don't blab to Dad." He quickly added, "If you blab, I'll know you're a real chicken. Bock, bock, BOCK!"

"Stop it!" cried Zeke, "I won't tell."

"Cool," said Griffin, grinning from ear to ear. Knowing they had a secret plan for later, Griffen was ready to head back to camp. He would figure out the details about how to scare the living daylights out of his brother later. "Let's hurry and get the firewood. Dad wants to go fishing. We don't want him to wonder where we've been."

"I'm going swimming, too," replied Zeke.

When the boys returned with the firewood, they saw that Dad had already put the boat in the water. They dropped the wood, grabbed their fishing poles, and ran to meet him.

After a long, lazy afternoon of fishing and swimming, they returned to the dock as the sun began to set on the horizon. Griffen was the first to exit the boat. He grabbed the rope to secure it and motioned for his brother to get out. Zeke pretended not to see him and took his sweet time. Zeke could tell that he was annoying his brother, but he felt it was payback for all the teasing about being a chicken.

"Wow! We sure did catch a lot of fish, didn't we?" said Zeke excitedly, as Dad handed him the bucket of fish.

"We sure did, son," responded Dad. "Actually, very surprising when you consider all the splashing you and Griffen did while swimming." They burst into laughter because they knew Dad was right.

As they walked back to their campsite, Dad assigned the chores. "Griffen, you start the campfire while Zeke and I clean the fish."

Griffen was good at building campfires. He enjoyed the challenge of building a fire using just one match. After layering kindling and starter twigs, he built a teepee out of larger pieces of wood around the kindling, making sure the structure was sturdy, yet would allow enough airflow to permit the fire to breathe. When he was satisfied with the placement of all the wood, he struck the match. He focused his entire attention on the fire for the next 10 minutes. When the flames were just right, he yelled out, "Fire's ready!"

With all their running, fishing, and swimming in the warm sunshine, all three were famished. Dad was an expert when it came to cooking fish on an open fire. The brothers watched as he seared one side of the fish and knew exactly the right time to turn and cook the other side without burning it. As Dad cooked the fish, the boys made sure that everything else was ready for dinner. After they had enjoyed their delicious meal, everyone joined in on the cleanup. This was mandatory. Dad wanted to make sure his sons understood that camping was fun, but that there were responsibilities as well.

"Make sure all the food is packed away and put in the truck," instructed Dad. "We certainly don't want any visitors sneaking into our camp tonight scavenging for food."

Zeke could feel his face turning red as Dad and Griffen looked at him. Suddenly they were all laughing, and they laughed even harder as Zeke retold the events of their last camping trip.

"I remember being woken up by a strange noise outside my tent. I was freaking out as I unzipped the tent to peak out. As soon as I did, this huge furry thing went running by!" recounted Zeke, as he threw his arms out to model the size. "I didn't mean to scream, but I thought for sure it was a bear. Then I heard Dad yell, 'Go on and get out of here!' I screamed again. I was so scared. I remember looking at you, Griffen, to see if you were awake, but you were sound asleep. I was going to wake you when I heard Dad say, 'It's okay, Zeke, it's just a couple of raccoons. They're looking for food, and they found it. Remember that third hotdog that you said you were too full to eat? Well, they found it right where you left it – on the picnic table.'"

"Yep," chimed Griffen towards the end of the laughter, "Zekey Boy strikes again!"

"Not funny…Griffen. How was I supposed to know that raccoons were going to come to the campsite looking for food? Especially for a hot dog!" He hated the nickname Zekey Boy.

"Duh! How many times do you have to be told to clean up after yourself? You always leave things lying around. Plus, Dad has told us a million times to take care of the food. But do you listen? No!"

"Okay, boys," interrupted Dad. "We need some more firewood. You two go." He studied his sons as he continued, "I'll finish the clean up and make sure all the food is taken care of. Make sure you don't kill each other

Lynette Teachout

while you're gone!" He knew the boys had to work out their differences in their own way, but a little peace and quiet would be nice, too.

Knowing they had just gotten out of doing dishes, the brothers wasted no time heading for the woods. Looking over his shoulder to check on his dad's whereabouts, Zeke whispered to his brother, "Do you want to go to the cemetery now?"

"No, Zekey Boy. It's not dark enough yet."

"Quit calling me Zekey Boy, Griffen. I don't like it! How would you like it if I called you Griffey Boy?"

With a smirk, Griffen replied, "Go ahead and see if I care. I'm not as sensitive as you are."

"Forget it," snapped Zeke. "Let's just get the firewood."

This time they took a different trail. Neither of them said a word while gathering the wood. Wanting to end the silence between them, Zeke was the first to speak, "Ready to tell your scary ghost stories tonight?"

"No can do," replied Griffen.

Surprised by his brothers' response, Zeke stopped and blurted, "Why not?"

Griffen could tell from the tone of his brother's voice that he was upset. He explained, "Dad thinks that you'll get too scared because of the dreams you're having about the Indian lady and that wolf."

"Really? What do your ghost stories and my dreams have to do with each other?" Zeke asked his brother.

"Beats me," said Griffen, shrugging his shoulders. "I'm just telling you what Dad said. You know I enjoy nothing better than telling you my super scary, ghoulish campfire stories. Muwah ha ha ha!" Griffen wiggled all ten fingers in Zeke's face.

"I know," laughed Zeke. "The one I like the best so far is the one with the two-headed, green monster who lived in the trees and flew around at night. You said it had been spotted the week before at the exact same campsite where we were camping. You said two kids, our ages, went missing. They put together a search party, but as of that night, those boys were still missing. You were pretty sure that the two-headed green monster had taken them. I wonder to this day if the search party ever found them."

Griffen smiled, "So you were listening! If I remember correctly, that was the same night the raccoons visited our campsite and scared the living daylights out of you. So much so, that you screamed, not once, but twice – just like a girl!"

"How would you know that I screamed twice? You slept through the whole ordeal. You slept like a log! The entire forest could have blown away in a storm and you wouldn't have heard it." They both chuckled because they knew Zeke was right. Griffen tended to sleep deeply.

"Anyway, Dad says no ghost stories tonight. It's getting dark and we need to get this firewood back to the campsite. Let's grab a couple more sticks and head back," said Griffen.

Zeke did as his brother suggested. After all, they were going to the cemetery later that night and that made up for the ghost stories. Maybe, just maybe, they would actually see a ghost. Just thinking about it sent a delicious chill down Zeke's spine.

As the brothers carried the wood back to the campsite, they plotted how they would sneak out of the tent to go to the cemetery. Griffen reminded his little brother not to tell Dad.

Not telling Dad made Zeke uncomfortable. Wasn't that the same as lying? Even if it was, he knew what Griffen was thinking. If he gave away their plan, Dad would stop them from going to the cemetery. Zeke really did want to go. Even though he was scared about going after dark, he was also excited. How cool would it be to tell all of his friends that he had seen a ghost? Plus he still had a gnawing feeling that this was something he needed to do. He had felt it since they first spotted the cemetery that afternoon.

Once the boys returned to the campsite they stacked the wood and joined Dad at the campfire. The conversation was nonexistent. Since Griffen wasn't allowed to tell any ghost stories, he really didn't have much to say. Plus, for some reason, Dad was unusually quiet instead of his usual talkative self. Typically, on their camping trips, Dad would ask them 50 questions to spark a conversation, or at least it seemed that way. He would ask questions about their friends, their plans for the upcoming week; their teachers and coaches, the cafeteria food. You name it and he would ask about it. Sometimes the conversation would turn to more serious subjects, like drugs, bullying, drinking, and how these things can impact your life. But tonight he was strangely quiet.

While sitting in silence, all Zeke could think about was going to the cemetery later. He tried to imagine what the adventure was going to be like. How scary would it be? He watched the flames of the fire flicker from orange to blue and back. As he watched, he could have sworn he saw the face of the Indian lady that he had been seeing in his dreams. But when he blinked, it was gone.

After sitting by the warm fire for more than an hour with nothing much being said, the day's activities began to take their toll. Dad was the first to start yawning, and before long they all were. Griffen was the first to announce that he was going to bed.

"Me, too," said Zeke.

"Goodnight, boys, don't stay up talking too long," said Dad, as he stirred the fire.

Chapter 2

Inside their tent, the brothers lay quietly on top of their sleeping bags. They listened as their dad moved around the campsite. Both were anxious to get started on their plan to visit the cemetery, but they knew they had to be patient. They had to wait until Dad finished checking on them, as they knew he would. He always did. Then they would have to wait until he fell asleep.

As tired as the brothers were from all the running, fishing and swimming, there was a growing sense of excitement about exploring their find from earlier that day. It certainly wasn't every camping trip that they found a cemetery, especially one that looked as old and mysterious as the one that they had discovered.

Zeke could feel his patience wearing thin. What was taking Dad so long? His curiosity was getting the best of him as he tapped on his brother's arm to get his attention. He wanted Griffen to know that he was going to get up and look outside to see what their dad was doing. As he started to rise, he felt his brother grab his arm. He turned to look at him. With just enough light cast from the campfire into the tent, Zeke saw his brother shaking his head "no." Although frustrated, Zeke remained still.

Griffen knew their dad's routine well and knew that his dad was just waiting for the campfire to burn down a little more. The fading smell of the burning wood and the diminishing glow of the campfire gave telltale signs that their wait wouldn't be too much longer.

A couple more minutes passed. Zeke couldn't stand it any longer. Ignoring his brother, he started to rise when he saw a shadow approach their tent. Quickly lying back down, he closed his eyes and pretended he was sleeping. He listened as Dad stood outside their tent. Sixty seconds later, he heard the zipper of his dad's tent being opened and then heard it being zipped shut again. "Finally!" he thought. Now they just had to wait for Dad to fall asleep.

All was quiet with the exception of the frogs croaking and crickets chirping. The brothers waited to hear one particular noise, the sound of Dad's snoring. Zeke and Griffen started giggling when they finally heard the all too familiar sound.

Zeke turned on his flashlight, casting a luminous glow inside the tent. "What time is it?"

Glancing at his cell phone, Griffen answered in a low whisper, "It's almost midnight. Are you ready?"

Zeke was ready, at least partly. Now that the adventure was about to start, he was suddenly having second thoughts. He had been so anxious to begin their adventure, but now part of him really just wanted to stay inside his cozy sleeping bag and forget about it. But then a strange feeling came over him. It felt almost like a pull, and he knew that visiting the cemetery was something that he was supposed to do. At the same time he felt guilty about sneaking out. "Are you serious? We're actually going to do this? You know we aren't supposed to!"

Griffen could feel himself becoming annoyed. Now was not the time to back out. He wanted to go and he wanted his brother to go with him. He certainly didn't want to go by himself. Deciding to give a little push, he responded, "I heard this cemetery has mystical powers! I'm going to check it out and you're coming with me!"

"Where did you hear that?" quizzed Zeke. "We didn't find the cemetery until today. Oh, wait, I know! One of the fish we caught today told you, right?"

Choosing to ignore the sarcastic comment, Griffen crawled out of the tent as quietly as he could. The one thing that he clearly understood about his brother was that he was a chicken at heart. There was no way Zeke would stay behind in the tent alone. Deep down Griffen knew that his brother would follow. Zeke proved him right, and once Zeke was outside the tent, Griffen leaned close to his brother's ear and whispered, "Be quiet and follow me. Stay close."

"Wait!" Zeke whispered back. "Do you have a flashlight?"

With a frown on his face and a growl in his voice, Griffen answered, "Yes, of course, and we have the light of the full moon," as he pointed up at the moon. Both brothers looked up at the moon and watched as the bright moonlit sky was darkened by a large cloud, covering the moon and diminishing its glowing light.

Satisfied, Zeke whispered, "Okay, I'm ready. Don't go too fast. I can't see you in the dark!"

Griffen turned on his flashlight and grabbed his brother's hand. They walked hand in hand until they reached the edge of the woods. Dropping his brother's hand, Griffen laid out the plan. "I'll lead from here, but I won't be able to hold your hand. This deer path is too narrow and we need to stay on the path in order to find the cemetery. Just stay behind me and stay close."

Zeke nodded his head up and down in agreement. He could feel his heart starting to beat faster. Suddenly, he realized that his palms were sweating. He wondered if they were sweating because he had been holding his brother's hand, or if it was because he felt nervous and excited.

As soon as the brothers entered the woods the light from the full moon disappeared. Zeke kept his flashlight pointed at the back of his brother's tennis shoes, while Griffen kept his flashlight pointed in front of him to light the deer path. It seemed to take forever before they found the bend in the path that indicated they were approaching the cemetery. Griffen stopped and pointed his flashlight to the left. His flashlight dimly illuminated the grave markers in the distance. Sure enough, there it was.

Griffen turned toward the cemetery, which meant they were leaving the path. As they emerged from the woods they both immediately noticed that the cloud cover had moved, allowing the moonlight to shine brightly again. As they looked around for the best way to approach the cemetery, Griffen shone his flashlight over what appeared to be ground that sloped down and then back up again. Moving forward slowly through the tall grass and brush, Zeke followed Griffen. Griffen wondered if they would have to walk through any mushy mud hiding underneath the tall grass, or worse yet, if there were any snakes hiding in the weeds. He knew from books that he read that most snakes hunted at night when it was warm. He hoped not, and he certainly was not going to tell his brother about his concerns.

They didn't have far to go, maybe a hundred yards or so. As they made their way down the slope of the land and through the tall weeds, they could feel the land gradually rising again. Finally, they reached a clearing close to the cemetery.

What they saw next surprised them both. The cemetery was surrounded by a tall iron fence that neither of them recalled seeing before. Griffen walked up to the fence to see if he could find an opening, or to see if there was a way for them to climb over. He swept the flashlight from side to side, then from the bottom of the fence all the way to the top. Once he reached the top he noticed that the decorative iron bars ended in a point. These points were at the top of every spindle, making it impossible for them to climb over. They would have to find a different way in.

Walking along the fence, searching for a way in, Griffen couldn't help but notice how eerie it all looked with the moonlight providing an almost iridescent shine to the iron railings. The fence made a sudden turn to the left. They continued to follow it until they found an entrance.

Stone pillars marked the small entrance. In the dark it did not appear wide enough to allow a car to drive through it. Perhaps a horse and buggy? Zeke's flashlight followed the stone pillars upward. He noticed there were words written with the same type of iron as the fence, but at the angle they were standing, he could only make out four of the letters, which spelled MOON. He started to back up to see what the rest of the letters spelled when he noticed that Griffen was starting to go through the cemetery entrance. Zeke reached out and pulled him back.

"Come on. I want to go in," complained Griffen.

Griffen misinterpreted the tugging and thought his brother wanted to leave. There was a part of him that just wanted to leave also, but he had not come all this way to chicken out now. He wanted to explore and he was not about to show his brother that he was even a little bit scared. Just for fun Griffen cupped his hands around his mouth and made a howling noise. With a low-toned growling voice, very slowly he asked, "Are you scared?"

"Yeah… Kind of…" answered Zeke softly.

"Well, get over it!" yelled Griffen. "We've come this far and you are not going to chicken out now!" Without any further hesitation Griffen turned and ran through the entrance of the cemetery.

It was times like these that made Zeke dislike his brother. He knew that he was just trying to be funny, but he wasn't. And now he felt like he had no choice. He could either stand on the outside of the cemetery by himself in the dark, which he was not about to do, or enter the cemetery and see where Griffen had run off to.

Once inside Zeke quickly found his brother, who was waiting for him just inside the entrance. He had turned off his flashlight, making it hard for Zeke to see him. For a split second Griffen thought about hiding and scaring his brother. But as he waited, he felt the same eerie feeling he had felt on the outside of the cemetery. It didn't help that there was a huge willow tree just inside the opening. The branches were long and dangly. The full moon's light gave them a shimmer that made them look alive. Griffen thought they looked as though they could grab hold of you and never let you go. "Stop it," he thought to himself. "No need to be scaring myself."

Slowly, with Griffen once again in the lead, they made their way through the dangly willow branches. Zeke stayed close. He thought of grabbing the back of Griffen's shirt to make sure he didn't take off again, but knew if he did that Griffen would make fun of him. When they emerged from the willow branches, Zeke was amazed at the scene.

He stood motionless as he watched small white balls of light moving swiftly in front of him. They zipped by, stopped, and zipped past again. At first there were only two white balls of light. They were soon joined by three green balls of light and then another white one. He couldn't believe what he was seeing. But, as weird as it was, he didn't feel frightened by them. He was just curious about what was causing them to appear. Standing frozen as he watched the light show, he didn't notice that Griffen had kept walking.

Likewise, Griffen hadn't noticed when Zeke stopped. Shaking off his initial fear, and thinking that his brother was right behind him, Griffen had kept walking. As he continued to let his flashlight guide his path, he suddenly felt the temperature change. Unexpectedly, he felt a really cold chill. "Did you feel that Zeke?" When his brother didn't respond, he turned around to see why. Zeke was still back by the willow tree. Griffen whispered loudly, "Come on, Zeke!"

Zeke looked in the direction of his brother's voice and was surprised to see several balls of light surrounding Griffen. "What are they?" he called out as he ran toward his brother. His face held an expression of excitement and mild alarm.

"What are what? You're not going to scare me, so don't even try," laughed Griffen.

"I'm not trying to scare you," responded Zeke. "I'm just amazed at how many there are and how fast they can move. And how fast they disappear and then appear someplace different."

"What are you talking about?" snapped Griffen.

"Those little balls of white and green lights that are everywhere," answered Zeke. They're all around you!"

"Oh, great! Now you're seeing creatures from outer space. Right…" snickered Griffen.

"No, I'm being serious, Griffen. Can't you see them?"

Becoming annoyed, Griffen sternly replied, "I didn't and don't see anything. You are such a nerd! Now, come on."

Zeke was getting tired of his brother's snippiness and ordering him around. It was taking all the fun out of exploring. He had just seen something that he had never seen before, and he was trying to figure it out. Suddenly, he remembered a dream that he'd had the week before. In that dream the Indian lady and the white wolf were in it. They had been surrounded by little white and green balls of light. Feeling completely freaked out now, he wanted Griffen to listen to him. "Griffen, stop!" hollered Zeke.

It was the tone in which Zeke yelled that made Griffen stop and turn around.

Excited, and freaked out about what he was remembering, Zeke blurted, "Remember the dream I had last week about the white wolf and the Indian lady?"

Griffen was irked and showed it. "How can I forget? You talk about it everyday. And once again you're bringing it up? You and those stupid dreams!" As soon as he said it, he wished he hadn't. He saw the disappointed and hurt look on his brother's face. He knew that Zeke's dreams had been freaking him out. Feeling bad, he quickly said, "Oh, yeah, I remember. Wasn't that the dream where you received the mystery message?"

Zeke's expression quickly changed from disappointed to puzzled, as he stammered, "There was a message in my dream." He stammered because he was trying to figure out if his brother was upset or interested. He was constantly running hot and cold. One minute they were laughing together and the next minute his brother was either yelling at him or making fun of him. It was really hard sometimes to figure him out. He chuckled to himself as he thought. "And he calls me weird!" He listened as Griffen continued.

"A message from the great beyond…" Griffen had put the flashlight up under his chin and was now making a horrible face. He knew that what he should be doing was convincing his brother that he cared. Actually he was so tired of hearing about the Indian lady and the wolf that he could scream. He didn't understand any of what Zeke told him about his dreams, so why waste time trying? It was just plain stupid.

"Stop It!" Upset with his brother's sarcastic remarks, Zeke turned to walk away. He had only taken two steps when he heard Griffen's startled voice say, "Wait! Did you hear that?"

"Hear what?"

Zeke thought to himself, "He's probably going to fart or something, thinking he's being so funny. Or he's going to do something to try and scare me." He waited for the sound but didn't hear anything, or smell anything. That meant Griffen must be trying to think of something to do to scare him. Not thinking either would be funny at this point, Zeke started to say, "Stop trying to scare me," but before Zeke could finish his sentence, he felt his brother's cold sweaty hand cover his mouth.

Zeke didn't move. His brother had never done anything like this before, and he wasn't sure what to think.

After a few seconds, he heard Griffen whisper franticly. "A voice … Like someone was talking to me. I just heard it again!"

"What's it saying? I can't hear it," whispered Zeke through his brother's fingers.

Zeke thought quietly, "If Griffen's telling me the truth, then why can't I hear it, too? Yep, I'm right. Griffen's trying to scare me."

Removing his brother's hand from his mouth and laughing out loud, Zeke replied, "You are such a nerd. Come on!"

"I'm being serious," demanded Griffen.

"Well, I was being serious about the balls of light!"

"Great! You're seeing things and I'm hearing them," responded Griffen. He wondered where the voice could be coming from. It was soft like a whisper and yet it sounded so close. Hearing the voice again, he quickly grabbed his brother's arm. "Sshh…there…there it is again. I can hear it again. It's saying, "Are you ready?"

Zeke looked at his brother like he was totally losing it. Still convinced that his brother was just trying to scare him, he responded with, "…for the light show?" Chuckling at his own joke, he turned to see Griffen's reaction. Based on the look on his face, Zeke knew he was really serious about trying to listen to whatever it was he was hearing.

Griffen exclaimed, "No, nothing about a light show. The voice is saying, "Some see, some hear, some feel."

"No way!" screamed Zeke. "You're messing with me!"

"No, I'm not. I promise." Very calmly Griffen reassured his brother that he was not messing with him.

Zeke asked Griffen to repeat what he heard.

Very slowly, Griffen said, "Some see, some hear, some feel."

Zeke couldn't believe what he had just heard. "Think back, Griffen, to when I told you about the message I had received in my dream. It's the same message! Some see, some hear, some feel."

Bewildered, Griffen's mind raced back to the dream conversation with his brother the week before. "You're right!" He shook his head in bewilderment. "Now that is just plain weird. Wonder what it means? Some see, some hear, some feel. Maybe I'm just remembering from what you told me last week."

Out of the corner of his eye, Zeke noticed balls of light starting to appear. Once again some of them were white and some were green. A few of the balls had a trail of light that followed them as they moved with extreme speed. As fast as they appeared, they would disappear. He said, "I don't know what it means.... I'm not hearing anything, but I'm seeing a bunch of light balls all around you. Want to hear something really weird?" he asked his brother.

"Not really," answered Griffen. Once again he could feel a cold chill around him. "I really am beginning to get freaked out. I think we should go!"

"Now who's being the chicken?" taunted Zeke, secretly wanting to leave too but not caring to admit it.

Griffen was not in the mood to argue with his brother, and more than willing to make his point. "I'm not turning into a chicken. I just don't like hearing voices when I don't know where they are coming from. I'm hearing things and you're seeing things! It's time to pack it in and head back!

Zeke could tell that Griffen had reached his limit. "Okay, let's go back."

As they turned to head back to the entrance, Zeke couldn't help but notice the different sized tombstones surrounding them. Tall ones, short ones, wide ones … they were all different sizes and shapes. He could just about make out some of the names on them as they walked by, but he did not dare stop to read any of the inscriptions. He knew that even the suggestion of stopping would bring words of disapproval from his brother.

They had almost reached the giant willow tree when Zeke once again noticed balls of light. This time they were moving in, out, and all around the willow tree. It was almost like he was watching fireflies blinking on and off, only these balls of white and green where much bigger than fireflies. What was really strange was that instead of being freaked out by them, he actually felt peaceful watching them. He liked watching how fast they could move in any direction and how they would suddenly appear and disappear.

He felt a push from behind as Griffen passed him and headed into the willow tree branches. Zeke scurried to keep up with his brother's quick pace.

Once they were outside of the cemetery, Griffen stopped and turned around to look back. Zeke shone his flashlight toward his face. He wanted to make sure his brother was okay. Griffen had a scowl on his face. It looked like he was really scared, but did not want to show it.

"You okay?" asked Zeke.

"Yes, I'm fine," answered his brother. "I just want to get back to camp."

"Are you still hearing a voice?"

"No." The answer was sharp.

"You don't need be snippy," pushed Zeke. "We'll just ask Dad about it. Maybe he can tell us what the mystery message means: Some see, some hear, some feel."

"Enough!" yelled Griffen. "I do not want to hear anything more about your dreams, mystery messages, balls of light, or voices. You understand? And you better not tell Dad."

"Don't yell at me. It was your idea to come to the cemetery after dark."

Calming himself down with a deep breath, Griffen walked up to his brother and put his arm around his shoulder. "I know the idea was mine, Bro, but I wasn't expecting all of this."

"What did you expect?"

With a sigh, his brother responded, "I don't know. We'd better head back. It's just a little too spooky for me."

"Yeah, I'm a little scared, too." Zeke smiled at his brother as Griffen walked away.

Neither brother saw the Indian lady watching them from the entrance of the cemetery. A white wolf sat next to her.

After they had exited the woods, Griffen reminded Zeke not to tell Dad about anything they had experienced that night.

Zeke thought for a moment and then promised he wouldn't. "But I want to know what that message means."

"I do too," said Griffen. "But right now, I'm tired. All I want to do is get back to camp and crawl into my sleeping bag. I'm exhausted."

Zeke laughed. "I don't know if I can sleep now. I'm too psyched up!"

Not wanting to use their flashlights as they got closer to camp, they both turned them off and let the moonlight guide them. Griffen had thought they would be able to see the campfire and would use it to help guide them back to their tent, but he couldn't locate any orange glow that would indicate they were nearing their campsite.

As they got closer to camp, they could make out the outline of the tents. Griffen noticed that the campfire had almost burned out. All that was left were some low burning embers. Not wanting the fire to go out entirely, he carefully added a few logs and stoked it back up.

While Griffen tended to the fire, Zeke crawled into their tent and directly into his sleeping bag. He had noticed on the way back that the night air had become damp but knew that between the tent and sleeping bag, he would be plenty warm.

Within a couple of minutes, Griffen joined him inside the tent and climbed inside his sleeping bag. He checked his cell phone for the time. It was 4:00 a.m. They had been gone for four hours.

"Hey, Bro, you sleeping?" whispered Griffen.

"Almost, why?"

"Do you think I really heard that voice?" questioned Griffen.

"Yes, I do. Do you believe me about the balls of light and my dream?"

"Yes, I guess so. I just wonder what it all means."

Still whispering, Zeke answered, "Since I can't ask Dad, I think I will ask my buddies when we get home. Maybe they will know."

Griffen chucked to himself. "I wouldn't do that, if I were you!"

"Why not?" questioned Zeke. "We need to ask someone, or how will we ever find out?"

Griffen hemmed and hawed for a minute. "Well, you can if you want to, but I don't think they will believe you. And I don't want you to tell them about me hearing the voice."

Feeling discouraged, Zeke pressed on. "You said you heard that the cemetery had mystical powers. Where did you hear that?"

"Bro, I just made that up to try and scare you. Believe me when I say none of my friends would have been talking about a cemetery that had mystical powers."

Exhausted from the long walk and the night's events, all Griffen really wanted to do now was sleep. He would think about it more in the morning. "Oh, yeah. It is morning," he thought as he whispered. "Night, Little Bro."

"Night, Big Bro."

Griffen rolled over inside his sleeping bag. Feeling bad about making fun of his brother's dreams, he rolled back over and whispered. "Zeke, if you have anymore dreams, promise me that you will tell me."

Smiling, Zeke responded, "I promise. I will."

Chapter 3

THE BOYS WERE SOUND ASLEEP in their tent. They never heard a sound as their dad awoke at his usual time. It was 6:00 a.m. After a few stretches, Dad was ready for some morning coffee. The boys had done a great job of gathering wood the day before, so all he had to do was walk over to the wood pile and grab a couple of pieces. He was expecting to have to restart the fire and was surprised to find hot embers still burning.

"One of the boys must have added some wood during the night," he thought to himself as he grabbed some logs. After he had added the wood, he waited for the fire to get hot. This was certainly a lot different than being home and waking up to coffee that was already made. He knew from experience that he would have to wait at least ten to fifteen minutes before the fire would be hot enough to boil water. As he waited for the fire to get hot, he kept himself busy by doing a few morning exercises. When he had finished, he grabbed the water kettle, went to the water jug and filled it with water. Next he grabbed his coffee cup and filled it with instant coffee.

The fire was ready. He placed the grate over the fire, set the silver water kettle on top, and waited for the water to boil. While waiting, he went to the truck and removed the cooler that was filled with eggs, bacon and everything he would need to make that morning's breakfast. After his second cup of coffee, he started breakfast. He knew that both sons had a hearty appetite, so he added the entire pound of bacon to the cast iron skillet.

Glancing at his watch, he was surprised to see it was already 7:30 a.m. If they were going to go fishing that morning, they had better get moving. By time they ate breakfast and cleaned up, half the morning would be gone.

He walked over to the tent to peek inside the window screen. There laid his two sons, sound asleep. He smiled to himself. They were good boys and he was very proud of both of them. "Hey boys, time to rise and shine." Seeing no movement, he called out their names. "Griffen... Zeke, time to rise and shine. You need to get up and around if you want to go fishing this morning." This time he watched through the screen as his sons slowly opened their eyes. Through his yawn, Griffen replied, "We're awake, Dad. We'll be out in a jiffy."

Satisfied that the boys were awake, Dad went back to campfire to continue cooking breakfast.

Slowly, Zeke crawled out from his sleeping bag and stood up. Looking down at his brother, he could tell that Griffen was in deep thought as he stared at the top of the tent.

"Whatchya doing?" asked Zeke. "You need to get up."

Griffen looked at his brother and whispered, "I'm thinking about last night. It just doesn't seem real."

Zeke sighed, "It was real alright. You heard a voice and I saw weird balls of light."

Griffen stared at his brother. His brain was trying to comprehend what had happened. It wasn't everyday that you had to admit that you were hearing voices. At least he hadn't seen any dancing balls of light like his brother. He wondered which was spookier. Slowly, Griffen crawled out of his sleeping bag and stood up. Facing his brother, he continued talking in a whisper, "I want to go back today."

Surprised, Zeke whispered back, "Why?"

"I want to see if what we experienced last night happens in the day time."

"Cool idea! Me, too! Are you going to ask Dad?"

Griffen paused. He didn't feel comfortable asking their dad to take them to the cemetery. He felt that his dad would ask too many questions. Questions like, "How did you find this cemetery?" And, "Why do you want to go this cemetery?" No, he didn't want to be put in that position. He thought it would be better coming from Zeke. "No, you ask him. But don't tell him what happened last night or even that we were there. Okay?"

Still whispering, Zeke agreed, "Okay, I'll ask him, and I won't say a word about last night."

"Good. And don't ask until we are fishing, okay?"

"Copy that," responded Zeke.

The boys quickly changed their clothes, replacing their jeans with shorts, and their t-shirts with clean ones. Leaving the tent, the smell of breakfast was a welcome greeting. "Grab your plates," said Dad. "Breakfast is ready."

Ten minutes later everyone was done eating and had started on the clean-up. With all of them working together, it didn't take long to put everything back where it belonged. Now it was time for some fishing.

They walked down to the water together. The boys waited while their dad untied the row boat. Griffen was the first to get in and sit down, followed by Zeke. Dad, who was ankle deep in water, was the last to jump in. The row boat swayed from side to side as Dad made his way to sit down. Balancing a row boat was something they were all aware of. Putting too much weight on one side of the boat would make it capsize. That was not what they wanted to happen.

Dad and Griffen rowed together while Zeke watched. He would have his turn rowing on the way back. He did have to admit that Griffen was better at rowing then he was, but Dad had always insisted that the only way to learn was to do it yourself.

When they found just the right spot, they stopped rowing and put down the anchor. Dad grabbed the anchor and slowly let it enter the water. Zeke watched the anchor as it disappeared into the darkness below. Depending on how clear and deep the water was, sometimes he would watch the anchor all the way until it hit bottom. Today would not be one of those days.

Lynette Teachout

After baiting their hooks, the day's fishing began. It wasn't long before Dad pulled in the first catch of the day. Re-baiting his hook, he was ready for the next catch. A few minutes later Dad had caught his second fish.

Zeke wasn't having the same kind of luck. He thought he felt a nibble a couple of times. He would draw his line taught by pulling back. He even brought the line all the way in, thinking that maybe a fish had eaten his bait, but that wasn't the case either. Actually, he wasn't concentrating on fishing at all. Instead he was thinking of how to best approach Dad about going to the cemetery later. Finally, he thought he had it all figured out and decided to start the conversation.

"Hey, Dad, I've got a question for you."

"Sure, son," replied Dad, as he remained seated with his back to his son, looking out over the water.

Zeke took a big breath and then asked his question. He felt nervous, but didn't know why. After all, it was just a question.

"Do you believe in ghosts?"

Dad took a minute, like he was thinking about how to answer. Griffen inwardly groaned. He would never have started the conversation that way.

"I don't know. I guess I never really thought about it," answered his dad frankly.

Zeke pushed on. "So, Dad, are you afraid of ghosts"?

"No, can't say that I am."

"What would you do if you ever saw a ghost?" Zeke knew that he had to be persistent, or Dad would just drop the conversation and that would be that.

Letting out a short chuckle, his dad shook his head, "Okay son. Why all the questions about ghosts? Did you have another dream about the Indian Lady?" Dad knew that there was a reason he was being asked these questions so he tried to just cut to the chase.

Before Zeke could respond, Dad felt a good tug on his line. Grabbing his pole tighter so that the fish wouldn't pull it into the water, he yanked

Journey with Zeke

back. Like an expert, he gradually pulled the fish toward the boat. He grabbed the fishing net and put it into the water to bring the fish out. Everyone was surprised at the size of the trout he hauled up. Dad quickly removed the trout from the line and placed it in the fishing bucket along with the other two. They would eat well tonight.

Zeke was the first to congratulate him, "Nice catch, Dad!" Then he added, "I'm just a little curious about ghosts. I thought it would be fun to go and explore this old cemetery that we found yesterday."

Dad had just cast his line back into the water. Slowly, he turned his head to the side to look at Zeke, and asked, "You found a cemetery?"

Griffen decided he would jump in before Zeke said something that he shouldn't. Even though Zeke had promised he wouldn't, Griffin wanted to be sure. "We did, Dad. We found it while we were looking for firewood yesterday."

"Interesting," said Dad. "You know there's a lot of history in a cemetery. After lunch, we'll walk over and explore. Who knows, maybe we'll see a ghost!"

Zeke and Griffen looked at each other and smiled. Griffen had to admit that the conversation went better than he expected and gave his brother a thumbs up. Zeke smiled from ear to ear. "Yep," he thought to himself. "Glad I didn't mess that up!"

From the reflection on the water and the heat of the sun, it was time to call it a day of fishing. They knew that the best time to fish was either early morning or late evening. Plus, Zeke had not caught any fish and was getting really bored. Griffen had caught three to add to the basket. So between Dad and Griffen, they had plenty of fish for dinner.

"Hey, I think it's time for some swimming," suggestion Griffen. He could tell that Zeke was getting really bored. He felt that he needed to reward his brother for the way he had handled himself that morning with their Dad.

Dad was the first to remove his shoes and socks, then his shirt. As he stood, the boat rocked back and forth a little bit, making the boys lose their balance as they were removing their shoes and socks.

"Last one in is a rotten egg!" yelled Dad, as he dove head first into the water. The boys quickly followed. The cold water felt refreshing after sitting in the hot sun. They spent the next twenty minutes teasing each other and swimming around. Feeling completely refreshed, Dad was the first to crawl back into the row boat. Griffen thought about tipping the boat over to make his dad fall back into the water, but remembered the fish, the fishing poles, the bait, and the clothes, so decided against it. As he made his way into the boat, Dad helped to balance it. When it was Zeke's turn, Dad helped him, too.

Zeke and Dad rowed the boat back to shore. Dad jumped out to secure the boat. Once the boat was secure, the boys got out. Griffen carried the fishing bucket as they headed to their campsite. They had already discussed that they would eat some lunch and then head to the cemetery.

When they were almost done eating, Dad asked, "How far away is this cemetery?" The brothers looked at each other. They weren't sure how to answer the question. They had been running down the deer path when they found it, and they sure didn't want to admit that they had snuck out of the tent the night before to go back. Even if they did admit that they had snuck out, they still couldn't really answer the question, because it was dark and they had relied on their flashlights to find their way there. Not sure what to say, Zeke looked at Griffen and waited for Griffen to answer the question.

"It's not far, Dad. We didn't go that far yesterday when we were looking for wood."

Dad nodded as he finished the last bite of his sandwich.

With the clean-up finished, the trio headed for the woods. Griffen took the lead, as he had the night before. When he reached the familiar deer path, he turned and led them into the woods. They all immediately felt the coolness of the shaded path.

As they walked, Dad started thinking about how his sons would react to walking into a cemetery. They had all been to a cemetery before, but the boys were really young and he was pretty sure that they did not remember going. It had been a long time since there had been the need to go to a cemetery.

Dad smiled to himself as he thought of the possibility of actually seeing a ghost. If truth be told, he didn't actually believe in ghosts. Therefore, he was really confident that they certainly would not see a ghost on this trip.

After careful thought he decided he would try to focus their attention on the tombstones and the history associated with them. He figured they would have a lot of questions.

As they neared the bend in the deer path, Griffen stopped.

"You lost son?" asked his dad.

"No, if I remember correctly the cemetery should be just around that bend up ahead," answered Griffen as he pointed in that direction.

"Okay, than let's keep moving. You're not getting scared are you?"

Griffen laughed, "Me, scared? No way!"

"Me neither," chimed in Zeke.

They continued to follow the path. Just like the two times before, when they rounded the bend, the cemetery came into view.

Dad's first thought was that he found it odd that the cemetery seemed to be in the middle of nowhere. He wondered how long it had been there and why he had never stumbled across it before. From the appearance of it, it had been there a very, very long time. There really was an eeriness to it.

"I wonder how you get in," questioned Dad. He noticed that there was a wrought iron fence that surrounded it. More importantly, he did not see an entrance.

"Let's cut across here," said Griffen as he turned toward the cemetery and ran down the slope through the tall grass and brush, just like he had the night before.

"Wait," said his dad. With all the tall grass, he could not see if there was water in what appeared to be a ditch, and he was not in the mood for walking through a bunch of muck or mud. "Let's walk down the path a little farther and see if we can find a better place to cross over. "

Griffen stopped. "It's okay, Dad." He was about to say that he and Zeke had been this way before. Realizing what he was about to do, he shut up.

Dad knew his sons were always up for adventure and felt that with their excitement to visit the cemetery they would walk through anything. "Come on, I'm not walking through that ditch. I'm sure there is higher ground further down. I don't want mud or muck all over our shoes," stated Dad, as he turned to continue down the path.

The brothers watched as their dad walked away. Zeke quickly made a face at his brother that said, "What did you almost do?"

Griffen smiled and shrugged his shoulders. He knew it had been a close call. He had almost slipped up. Walking back up the slope that he had started down, he couldn't help but think how hard it is to cover up something that you know you shouldn't have done. Lying was hard work. It was a feeling that he was not used to, and did not like.

When he reached the top of the slope, the boys ran to catch up with their father. As they turned the next bend in the path, they found where indeed the ground was level and made for easy crossing to the cemetery. In fact, all they had to do was follow the deer path and it led them directly to the entrance of the cemetery.

"Zeke, have you seen a ghost yet?" teased his father as they approached the entrance.

Zeke laughed, "Yeah, Dad, I've seen a couple. Haven't you?"

Griffen let out a loud "Boo", as he ran up behind his brother and grabbed him around the shoulders.

"Funny, Griffin! You're going to have to do better than that if you're going to scare me!"

"Boys, listen to me for a moment. By the looks of this cemetery it's really old. That means that there is a lot history behind that fence. When we go in let's see who can find the oldest tombstone."

"Really, Dad, you know I don't care too much for history," joked Griffen. Actually history was one of Griffen favorite subjects, and his dad knew it. What he and his father also knew was that history was not one of Zeke's favorite subjects. They both looked at Zeke and awaited his response.

Zeke knew what they were up to and wasn't going to fall into their trap. He looked back at them, smiled and said, "Come on. Let's go find the oldest tombstone."

Just like the night before, the first thing the trio had to do was maneuver through the willow tree branches that were hanging so low that some of them actually touched the ground. Only this time, Zeke did not see any white or green balls of light. As they emerged on the other side of the branches they could see about a hundred tombstones to explore.

Zeke ran ahead as he called out, "I'm going to start at the far end and work my way back to you, Dad." Dad smiled. He loved that his son was getting into it. "Okay, son, you do that. I'll start up here," responded his dad. "Griffen, you start somewhere in the middle."

Everyone started yelling out dates. "1901!" "1898!" "1896!" "1906!" "1889!"

"Hey, Dad," yelled Zeke. "You were right. This is a really old cemetery." As they continued to yell out the dates, they all noticed that some of the tombstones were really hard to read. Some were covered with green moss and some were broken off or crumbling so badly that any wording was lost. On others, the lettering was so worn that it was only a faint impression on the stone.

As Zeke made his way back toward the front, reading and yelling out dates, he finally reached a tombstone that was much bigger than the rest. He called for his brother and Dad to come see it.

While he was waiting for them, he read what was engraved on the front of the tombstone:

MOON WILLOW
Forever in our Hearts
1800 to 1836
Take a willow stick home and
place it under your pillow.

Zeke had just finished reading the inscription when Dad and Griffen joined him. Dad read the inscription aloud:

MONA WILLIAMS
Forever in our Hearts
1800 to 1836
May the spirit of many blessings
travel with you on your journey

With a confused look on his face, Zeke looked at his father. Thinking that his dad was trying to play a joke on him, he waited until he finished reading the entire inscription.

"Funny, Dad! That's not what it says."

Griffen looked at Zeke like he had lost his mind. "Yes, it does. Don't you know how to read? It says exactly what Dad just read. What are you talking about?"

Zeke had turned to look at Griffen as he was arguing with him and turned back to the tombstone to read it again. To his complete surprise the wording he saw before was gone, and he was now seeing what his dad had read aloud. Stumped, he quickly apologized.

"It's alright, son. Some of these inscriptions are really hard to see. "So, what did you think you read?"

"Yeah, Zeke, what did you think you read?" taunted Griffen. "I mean, you would have to be blind not to be able to read that inscription. I agree with Dad some are hard to read, but not this one!"

Dad quickly threw Griffen a look that said "you better knock it off." Griffen saw the look and smiled as he shook his head at Zeke.

Flustered by what had just happened, Zeke just put his head down and mumbled, "Never mind."

"Okay, I think it's time for us to head back. We have to break down the camp and get everything packed. Your mom is expecting us home in time for dinner." Dad slowly walked away and Griffen followed. Zeke lingered at the tombstone. He wanted to read that darn inscription one more time. Once his brother and Dad were up the path a little way, he directed his attention to the tombstone. He was astonished to see that the inscription was now the same as what he had originally read:

MOON WILLOW
Forever in our Hearts
1800 to 1836
Take a willow stick home and
place it under your pillow.

Wanting to call his brother and Dad back, he looked to see where they were. He immediately spotted Dad, but couldn't find Griffen. Then he felt something touch his leg, making him jump.

"Gotchya!" laughed Griffen.

Usually Zeke would have been angry with his brother, but not this time. Instead, he was glad Griffen was there. "Griffen, listen to me. I'm not making this up or fooling around. I read something different than what you and Dad did. I just saw it again. Do you see it?"

Griffen could tell that his brother was being serious. Curious, he looked at the tombstone. When he did, he heard a voice say. "Take a willow stick home and place it under your pillow."

Puzzled, he looked at his brother, "Did you just say something?"

"No, I'm waiting for you to tell me what you see on that tombstone." Griffen looked at the tombstone, but before he could read the inscription, once again he heard a voice say, "Take a willow stick home and place it under your pillow."

Griffen jumped. Annoyed, he yelled at Zeke, "That's not funny so just stop it!"

"Stop what?" snapped Zeke.

"Stop making that voice! Now that I think about it, you were probably making that voice I heard last night too!"

"I don't know what you're talking about Griffen! Seriously! I'm not making any voice!"

Griffen took a deep breath. "Okay, then. Bro, I'm telling you that I just heard a voice tell me to take home a willow stick and place it under my pillow. Did you hear it?"

"No! No, I didn't, but that is exactly what I read on the tombstone! And the name was different. It wasn't Mona Williams, it was Moon Willow."

"Seriously, Bro, you're not lying to me?"

"I promise you. Cross my heart and all that stuff that I'm not lying to you."

Griffen closed his eyes and shook his head slowly. "Great – it's official, I'm ready for the looney bin. So now what? Do we take a willow stick home and put it under our pillow?" he asked.

"Why not? What could it hurt? I say we do it," encouraged Zeke.

Mystified and spooked, Griffen just wanted to leave. He was beginning to regret visiting the cemetery. If he really was hearing this voice, then what would happen if he actually listened to the voice and took home a willow stick? Maybe the willow stick was part of a curse or something. Not knowing what to do, he ignored his brother's encouragement and instead replied, "We better get going. Dad's waiting for us."

As the brothers made their way to the entrance of the cemetery, Griffen eyed the giant willow tree. He was waiting to hear the voice again, but all was silent. As they neared the tree, he looked around on the ground and saw several fallen willow sticks. Feeling a little silly now about being afraid, he bent down and picked one up. Zeke did the same.

Dad was happy when he saw his sons finally walking his way. He had been watching them from the entrance of the cemetery. He could tell by their body language that they had been having an intense conversation. Perhaps Griffen was apologizing for sneaking back around and scaring his brother. Whatever it was, he was going to let the two of them work it out.

"Hey, Dad, we're going to take home a souvenir from our adventure today," said Zeke with a smile.

"No, you're not," replied his dad. "You should never remove anything from a cemetery. Cemeteries are sacred ground. To remove anything or to destroy anything is very disrespectful."

Dad's tone had been so stern that it took the boys by surprise. However, Zeke was determined that he was going to take home a willow stick. "Dad, I would never be disrespectful to a cemetery. When I said souvenir, I was referring to a willow stick."

Completely puzzled, his dad looked at him with a strange expression on his face. "A willow stick! Why in the world would you want to take a willow stick home?"

"Because I think it would be neat. Who knows, Dad, maybe a willow stick holds some kind of magical power."

Dad chuckled. He never knew what was going to come out of Zeke's mouth. What he did know was that his son had a great imagination.

"Okay, you can take home a willow stick. Just make sure you don't pick one off of the tree, and hurry up. We need to get going."

Dad was surprised when he noticed Griffen also holding a willow stick. He found it very odd, but didn't say anything. Now that both boys had their willow sticks, they all walked out of the cemetery the same way they had entered.

Back on the deer path, Zeke said, "Hey, Dad, did you see any ghosts?"

"Nope, didn't see any ghosts. Did you?"

"No, but I wish I had. I think it would have been fun." Zeke turned around to get one last look at the old cemetery. That's when he noticed, for the first time, the full name of the cemetery. Written in the same wrought iron as the fence were the words, "Moon Willow Cemetery".

He was shocked. He came to a sudden stop and without saying a word he looked at his brother and then pointed to the entrance of the cemetery. Griffen turned to see what he was pointing at. Zeke watched as his brother's mouth dropped open and his eyes grew big. But that was nothing compared to what happened next.

Zeke turned to look back at the cemetery name and that is when he saw it – a ghost-like figure of an Indian lady dressed in a long tan dress. She had a headband around her head. She looked just like the Indian Lady that he had seen in his dreams. She was standing in the entrance of the cemetery and by her right side was a white wolf. He couldn't believe what he was seeing. He quickly took a step forward to get a better look. When he did, they vanished.

"What are you boys doing?" hollered Dad. Both boys looked at their father and ran to catch up with him. Zeke wanted to tell him in the worst way what he had just seen, but with all the joking about seeing ghosts, he already knew that Dad wouldn't believe him. So he didn't say anything.

On the walk back to the campsite, Dad pointed to different trees and asked the boys to name them. It came as no surprise to him that the boys knew all the trees by name, even the pine trees that came in a variety of different species.

Once they arrived back at camp, the boys quickly took down the tents while Dad loaded the boat onto the boat trailer. When he returned, everything was packed. They loaded all of their gear into the truck.

Dad took a look around to make sure they hadn't forgotten anything. He also wanted to make sure that the area was just as clean as when they had arrived. Nothing was more irritating than arriving at a campground to find that the previous campers had left a mess. Not that where they had stayed last night was a campground. Actually the land and the lake were owned by a guy he had gone to school with. He would be sure to ask Ray about the cemetery when he called to thank him for letting them camp there.

Satisfied, he jumped into the truck, reached for the radio, found a radio station that played oldies music, and started home.

Chapter 4

ZEKE WAS HAPPY TO BE riding in the back seat on the way home. It gave him time to think about everything that had happened in the last twenty-four hours. If he had sat in the front seat Dad would have talked to him all the way home. He was afraid that he would mess up like Griffen almost did and say something about going to the cemetery the night before. As he thought about seeing the white and green balls of light, and about Griffen hearing the strange voice, he could feel his eyes getting really heavy.

Dad could see his son in the rearview mirror and noticed that he was starting to fall asleep. He was a little worried about him. It just seemed that lately he had this obsession with ghosts, an Indian Lady, and strange dreams. He wasn't sure what to make of it all. There was a part of him that believed it was typical teenage stuff. Then again, Griffen had never gone through anything like this. He wondered if he should sit down with his son and have a heart to heart talk.

A few minutes later Dad checked the rearview mirror again. Sure enough, his youngest son had fallen asleep. He looked over at Griffen and saw that he, too, looked like he was falling asleep. Not knowing if there would be enough time to talk to him at home, Dad started the conversation. "Griffen, has Zeke mentioned anything more to you about his dreams, an Indian Lady, a white wolf, or anything else along those lines?"

Griffen jerked awake. He wasn't sure that he had heard Dad's entire question and asked him to repeat it. This time he listened carefully.

"Yes, he's told me numerous times."

"Did you two watch a scary movie about a ghost, or one of those reality ghost shows?" quizzed his dad.

Griffen thought for a minute. Shaking his head, he replied, "Dad, I can't think of anything unusual." He wondered if he should tell Dad about going to the cemetery the night before, but thought better of it. Whatever was going on with his brother had started before this trip. Besides, Zeke wasn't the one who was hearing a voice, he was. There was a part of him that wanted to ask his dad about the voice, but he was too tired. All he wanted to do right now was sleep.

Dad looked over at his oldest son and saw that he too had fallen asleep. Left with no one to talk to, he turned his full attention back to the road. He kept the volume low and when he started singing along to the tunes, it was more like a quiet hum.

Glancing at the truck's clock, he realized why he was feeling hungry. They had been on the road now for almost two hours. It was already after noon. He knew the route well and knew that he didn't have far to go before they would reach one of his favorite restaurants. He reached over and shook Griffen's shoulder. "You ready for some lunch?"

"Sure, Dad," answered Griffen as he stretched and repositioned himself in the seat.

After calling Zeke's name three times, and continuously glancing at his rearview mirror, he saw that Zeke had opened his eyes. "You ready for some lunch, son?"

Zeke blinked his eyes a couple of times as he woke up. In a groggy, quiet voice he answered, "Yeah."

Five minutes later Dad turned into the Schum's parking lot. Jumping out of the truck and skipping toward the restaurant, Zeke was the first one to reach the door. As he held the door for his brother and father, he couldn't help but notice the delicious hamburger aromas emanating from the restaurant. They made his stomach growl.

They had been to this restaurant before, but it had been a really long time ago. Dad led them to a table back in the corner. What the boys did not know was that Dad had purposely planned to stop at Schum's all along. He had something very delicate that he wanted to talk to them about.

They each placed their order for a Schumburger, fries, and a soda. After the waitress left, Dad smiled at his sons. "Hope you two had a good time. I know I did. I always enjoy camping and fishing with you both."

"I had a great time Dad, and I'm looking forward to the fish fry tonight," responded Griffen.

"Me too Dad," chimed in Zeke. By the way did you let Mom know that we caught lots of fish and we're having a fishing fry tonight? You know how she likes fish!" Griffen and Dad nodded in agreement. Deciding that now was the time, Dad began.

"No, I didn't. I thought we would surprise her. Speaking of Mom, I have something that I want to share with you boys." The boys watched as their dad took a deep breath before he continued. "Your mom is going to be going away for a little while. Grandma B is sick again and your mom is going to fly to Florida to be with her." He paused and took a second to look at each son. "I really need both of you to be strong for your mom and grandma, okay? Mom feels bad about leaving, but knows this is something that she has to do." Stunned by what they had just heard, both of the boys sat still, waiting for their dad to continue. They could tell that he was struggling to find the right words. Griffen knew that whatever it was, it wasn't going to be good news. He knew from what Dad had already said what it must be. He decided to just ask the question.

"Dad, is Grandma B's cancer back?"

"Yes, son, I'm afraid it is."

Zeke could feel tears welling in his eyes. He didn't want to cry, but couldn't help it. Seeing the tears in Zeke's eyes, his dad reached out and took his hand.

"I know it's scary. We'll continue to keep Grandma B in our prayers. She beat cancer once before and we'll pray that she does again."

"What happens if she doesn't, Dad?" questioned Zeke.

"We're not going to think that way right now," answered his dad. "Instead, we all need to think positive and be positive. Grandma B is in good hands. She has some really good doctors that will do anything and everything they can."

"Can we go see her, too?" asked Griffen.

"Not right now, son. Just Mom is going to go. Once Grandma B is feeling better again I promise that she will either come here to see us, or we will go to Florida to see her. Right now she'll need all of her strength to heal herself. I know you both would want that for her. You can get her a card, write her a note, call her, or whatever you're comfortable doing. I know she would love to hear from her two favorite grandsons."

Their conversation was interrupted by the delivery of lunch. Just wanting to get home to see his mom, Zeke quickly ate his burger and fries. Soon after, Dad and Griffen also finished eating.

Dad left a tip on the table and went to the cashier to pay the bill. The boys went ahead to the truck. Just like before, Griffen sat in the front seat, while Zeke sat in the back. Neither one said a word about Grandma B. A few minutes later they were on the road heading home.

"We're home, Mom!" called Zeke, as he burst through the kitchen door. He quickly tossed his sleeping bag and his duffle bag down on the floor. "Mom," he yelled, "Where are you?"

When he didn't hear a response, his stomach dropped with disappointment. "Maybe she's already gone," he thought. He yelled again, "Mom, we're home!"

Griffen, also carrying his sleeping bag and duffle bag into the kitchen, was right behind him. "Gee man, can you yell just a little louder so that all the neighbors can hear you?" he snapped.

"Griffen, be nice to your brother," his dad said softly.

Griffen rolled his eyes at his dad. His dad responded with a firm look that Griffen understood well. It meant don't be disrespectful and stop with the snippy remarks.

"Hey, there are my boys," said Mom, as she entered the kitchen.

Instantly, Zeke ran to his mom and gave her a big hug and kiss. Smiling, she returned the hug and kiss, asking, "How was your camping trip?"

"It was so much fun, Mom," answered Zeke excitedly. "We visited a cemetery!"

"Really?" replied Mom looking over to Dad. "I thought you were going fishing."

Everyone laughed as Griffen crossed the kitchen to give his mom a hug.

"We did, Mom," said Griffen, "and we also visited a cemetery."

Mom returned the hug and planted a kiss on Griffen's cheek, all the while looking at their dad with a confused look on her face.

Dad was next to get a hug and kiss. The boys noticed the wink when he said "Hi Honey. We'll tell you all about the cemetery visit at the fish-fry tonight."

Mom had a twinkle in her eye as she smiled. "Ah, so you did catch a lot of fish. I was hoping you would. Okay, boys, take your stuff upstairs and bring down your dirty clothes. That goes for you, too," she said, winking back at Dad.

Picking up his duffle bag, Zeke went directly to his room. He sat the bag down on his bed, unzipped it, and then dumped the contents onto the floor. He already knew that all the clothes needed to be washed. There was the faint smell of perspiration and fish in the room. He quickly scanned his entire bedroom for more dirty clothes, and then went to the bedroom closet to check the hamper. On his way back to pick up the clothes from the floor, he noticed the willow stick lying next to them. Remembering the wording on the tombstone, he placed the willow stick under his pillow. He wondered if Griffen would remember to do the same thing.

Zeke threw his dirty clothes into the basket and headed to his brother's room. As soon as he entered he looked for the willow stick, but did not see it. He asked Griffen, "Did you put your willow stick under your pillow?"

Griffen was gathering his dirty clothes. He answered with an abrupt, "No!"

"Are you going to?"

"I don't know. I've got other things on my mind."

Zeke knew when it was a good idea to clear out and give his brother space. This was one of those times. "Okay. Give me your clothes and I'll take them to Mom."

Griffen quickly gathered his clothes and handed them to his brother. Once his brother had left the room, Griffen lay down on his bed. "Cancer," he thought.

It wasn't that long ago when they had visited Grandma B in Florida. It had been a special trip in more ways than one. Grandma B had found out that she was in remission and they had gone to visit the Harry Potter Theme Park at Universal Studios. He had a blast. Hogwarts was so cool and it was exactly the way it had appeared in the movies! It had been a trip to remember. Now Grandma B's cancer was back. He couldn't take it any longer. He lay his head down on his pillow and let the tears flow. Ten minutes later, he wiped his eyes, jumped out of bed and headed for the garage.

Out in the garage, Dad and Zeke had the fish lying out on newspaper spread over a table. Cleaning fish could be messy and no way did Mom want the fish cleaned in the house. She would always say, "Smelling fish is one thing; cleaning fish in the house is something completely different."

"What do you want me to do?" asked Griffen when he reached the table.

"Why don't you help Zeke clean the fish while I fillet them?" answered Dad. Within the hour, they had cleaned and prepared all the fish. They happily passed them over to Mom to prepare for dinner.

After dinner, Mom filled them in on what she knew about Grandma B's cancer. Although not sure how long she would be gone, she knew for sure that she would be leaving on Monday.

"That means we only have tomorrow to spend with her before she leaves," thought Griffen.

After Mom had answered all the questions that she could, she asked everyone to join hands and say a silent prayer for Grandma B, which they did. Mom looked at the three main men in her life, and with a smile, she reassured all three that they were going to get through this okay. That she didn't want them to worry about something that they had no control over.

After Mom had finished reassuring everyone, Dad announced that there was a new comedy movie coming on. Feeling that they all needed some laughter right now, he nodded his head towards the living room and said, "Let's go watch it."

The movie was exactly what they all needed. It took their minds off of Grandma B.

For the next 90 minutes they laughed and laughed again. When the movie ended, Zeke stood. Even though he had slept on the way home from Mystic Lake, he was still tired. He let out a loud yawn and announced, "I'm going to bed. I'm whipped."

"Me too," said Griffen, as he stood and walked over to his mom. It was their bedtime ritual to give each parent a hug and to say "I love you". It was such a natural thing to do, and when Griffen hugged his mom, he realized that he would only be hugging her for one more night before she left. He was about to tell her that he was really going to miss her when he heard "Beat you upstairs!"

Zeke laughed as he ran for the stairs.

"Next time, Bro," answered his brother as he headed for the kitchen. "I'm going to get some milk. My stomach feels a little weird."

"And you're going to drink milk? Whatever," said Zeke as he turned to head up the stairs.

Chapter 5

WHEN ZEKE REACHED THE TOP of the stairs, he decided to wait for his brother. He sat on the middle of the top step knowing Griffen would have to stop or go around him. He wanted to make sure Griffen had placed his willow stick under his pillow.

As soon as Griffen started up the stairs, he noticed Zeke. "Why couldn't he just have gone to bed?" he thought to himself. He wasn't in the mood for any of Zeke's games tonight. He didn't want to hear anything about his dreams, or that stupid willow stick. He had enough on his mind. He was tired and worried about Grandma B.

Griffen slowly walked up the stairs until he faced his brother. It was everything he could do not to knock him over and keep going. He certainly wasn't going to be nice and say, "Excuse Me," especially since he knew his brother was purposely blocking him. "What do you want?"

"I wanted to know if you put the willow stick under your pillow."

Griffen rolled his eyes and continued past his brother. "I haven't yet."

Zeke jumped up to follow his brother down the hall. He wasn't about to let this go. "Griffen, you heard a voice tell you twice to place the willow stick under your pillow, so why haven't you? I mean come on. How hard is it to just put the willow stick under your pillow? Aren't you the least bit curious?" Even though Griffen glared at him, he continued to push. "You gonna?"

Now standing just outside his bedroom door, Griffen stopped, spun around, and growled. "Don't worry about that stupid willow stick!"

Zeke wasn't surprised by Griffen's response. He usually became grouchy when he was tired or didn't feel well. "Fine, you don't have to be such a grouch."

Ignoring his brother, Griffin continued into his bedroom and slammed the door. Zeke debated if he should follow. He had his hand on the door knob but he thought better of it. "Better not," he thought to himself. "It will just make him even grouchier." Instead, he went to his own room and closed the door.

Zeke looked at the clock that sat on the table next to his bed. It read 9:45 p.m. Even though he was physically tired, he was wide awake. He changed into his pajamas and crawled into bed. He reached over and turned off the lamp, bathing the room in darkness. He stared at the ceiling, letting his eyes adjust. After a couple of minutes, he noticed the soft moonlight of the full moon filled the otherwise dark room. Reaching under his pillow to feel the willow stick, he slowly drifted off to sleep.

Zeke awoke suddenly. He was confused. Sitting up in bed, he blinked his eyes. He focused to make sure his eyes were not playing tricks on him. Still not convinced, he slowly crept out of bed and went to his bedroom door. He quickly opened and then shut the door behind him and went directly to his brother's room. Griffen's door made a slight creaking sound as he gently opened it. He didn't bother to close the door behind him. Making his way over to his brother's bed, he began nudging him and urgently whispered, "Griffen, wake up! Wake up!"

Griffen didn't understand why he felt his body shaking. He shrugged his shoulders to make it stop, but then he heard his brother's urgent whispers. "You've got to be kidding me," he thought. Angrily he snipped, "What? Leave me alone!"

Zeke leaned closer to his brother. He didn't want to wake his parents, but he wanted to be sure that Griffen heard him, "You've got to see this!"

Something in the tone of his brother's voice brought Griffen to his senses. Curiously, he asked his younger brother, "See what?"

"My room is glowing!" replied the excited voice.

"No kidding," responded Griffen. "There's a full moon tonight, remember? What time is it, anyway?

"3:00 a.m.," answered Zeke, as he grabbed his brother's arm to pull him out of bed. "Come on, you've got to see this!"

Griffen got out of bed and followed his brother quietly to his room.

Zeke slowly opened the door. As soon as he did a luminous haze started to appear. He continued to slowly open the door until it wouldn't open any further. Inside, the entire room was glowing. It was a bright, luminous, yet soft glow.

Griffen could not believe what he was seeing. "Where is that light coming from?"

Zeke turned around, smiling from ear to ear, and answered, "The willow stick!"

"No way, Bro. Are you sure?"

"I don't know what else would make this kind of light. It makes sense. I put the willow stick under my pillow when we got home yesterday. Last night before I fell asleep, I checked, and it was still there. A few minutes ago I woke up to this light and came to get you."

Zeke started to enter the room. Griffen quickly grabbed his arm, "Don't go in."

"Why?" questioned Zeke. "I came out of the room. I think I can go back in. Besides, how can I check the willow stick if I don't go back in? I don't think the light will hurt me."

Griffen thought for a minute. "Okay, I'm right behind you."

Zeke went to his bed and lifted his pillow. There lay the willow stick, but he couldn't tell if the light came from it or from some other source. It was really weird. This awesome light engulfed the entire room, yet he had no idea how or where it actually came from.

"Is it the willow stick?" questioned Griffen.

"I don't know. I can't tell." Zeke watched as his brother looked up to make sure that the overhead light wasn't on. Next, he went to the window to see if anything from outside was making the light. He could not find anything that would make this type of light. When he was done with his search, Griffen moved back to the middle of the room. He raised his hand directly out in front of him to see if the light would do anything? He didn't notice the light changing. But he did feel something.

"Zeke, do you feel what I feel?"

"I don't know. What are you feeling?"

Griffen smiled and explained, "I feel happy – extremely happy….and warm. I don't know how else to describe it."

Zeke stood still for a moment and thought about what his brother described. Now that he mentioned it, he, too, was experiencing the same feeling. "Yeah, I feel it, too. I wonder if your room is glowing. Did you put the willow stick under your pillow?"

"No, I never did, but let's go check it out."

The boys left Zeke's room and headed back to Griffen's room. When they got there the room was dark, except for the moonlight. "I wonder why my room isn't glowing like yours."

"Where's your willow stick?" questioned Zeke.

"I'm not sure. I was upset with you bugging me about it, so I threw it off the bed."

Zeke started to reach for the bedroom light. "Don't turn that on", whispered Griffen. "The light might wake Dad and Mom."

"I'll shut the door first."

"Go ahead and shut the door, but don't turn on the light. We can find the stick. Just get down on your hands and knees and feel for it. There's enough light from the moon that it shouldn't be too hard."

Zeke quietly shut the door and both boys dropped to their hands and knees and started feeling around. "Let me know if you find it."

"Nope, I'm going to keep it a secret," said Griffen sarcastically.

"Funny," said Zeke.

They continued searching the floor. Zeke touched something that felt like a stick. Picking it up, he held it toward the window to see it better. Griffen noticed and crawled to the center of the room to join his brother.

"Let me see it," said Griffen. Zeke handed the object in his hand to his brother. Just as Griffen lifted the object up to get a closer look, the room went completely dark. Both boys froze, waiting for a light to appear from the object. Some light finally returned to the room. Griffen started laughing. Zeke gave him a questioning gaze.

Griffen pointed to the window and leaned closer to his brother, as he whispered, "The moon."

"What does that mean?" whispered Zeke, as he strained to see his brother's face. The room had suddenly gone dark again.

"The moon went behind some clouds making the room dark. That's all it was."

Zeke didn't know if he should sigh with relief or be disappointed that nothing mystical happened. "Okay, so is that the willow stick?"

Griffen held the object in his hand back up to the window. There was enough moonlight for him to see that he was not holding the willow stick. Instead, it was his drum stick. "No, but it's got to be here. We just need to find it."

They continued searching the floor on their hands and knees. This time Zeke's knee felt the pain of something that he had just knelt on. "Ow!"

"Sshh! You're going to wake Mom and Dad," reminded Griffen.

"Sorry. I think I really did find your willow stick this time." Zeke lifted his knee and handed the object to his brother.

Once again Griffen held the object in his hand up to the window. "Yep. This is it."

"Cool, but why isn't it glowing like mine?" whispered Zeke.

"I don't know what to tell ya, Bro. Maybe only your willow stick has magical powers," snickered Griffen.

"Not funny, Griffen."

"I know, just trying to have a little fun to lighten the mood."

"Maybe you should put the willow stick under your pillow, the way I did," suggested Zeke.

Journey with Zeke

"Good idea." Griffen crawled over to his bed and lifted the pillow. As soon as he placed the willow stick under the pillow, he heard a voice. Startled, he fell backwards onto the floor with a yelp.

"What are you doing?" questioned Zeke. "You told me to be quiet!"

"Bro, I just heard a voice."

"Funny, Griffen. You're not going to scare me, so just stop it!"

"I'm not trying to scare you. I'm telling you the truth. I swear!"

"What did the voice say?"

Griffen repeated what he had heard. "Dude, it said, 'Are you ready?'"

"Are you ready for what?"

"How would I know?, stammered Griffen. But you want to hear something freaky?" Griffen reminded his brother that those were the same words that he heard at the cemetery.

Zeke's eyes grew big as his mouth dropped open. "That's right. I remember now!" Zeke quickly stood up. Let's take your stick to my room. If my room is still glowing, maybe yours will glow or you'll hear something else." Griffen stood to follow his brother. Opening the door a crack, Zeke peeked down the hall to his room. Now it was dark.

"Is it still glowing?" questioned Griffen.

"No, it's dark."

"Okay, shut the door and turn on the light. I want to take a closer look at the willow stick. Maybe there is some secret to this and I'm missing it."

Zeke quietly shut the door. After it was closed, he turned on Griffen's bedroom light. Any thought of waking their parents flew out the window. This inspection was worth it.

Griffen sat down on the side of his bed and carefully inspected the willow stick. When he was finished he handed it to Zeke. "Look and see if you notice anything."

"What am I looking for?" questioned Zeke.

"I don't know. Just do it."

Zeke carefully inspected the willow stick. He ran his hand along every inch, feeling for trick levers or knobs. Nothing happened. Stumped, he placed the willow stick between them as he sat down next to his brother.

Still whispering, Zeke told Griffen that he had been having another dream about the Indian lady and her white wolf when he woke up and saw the white light in his room. This dream had been different from his prior dreams. This time in the dream they were at Grandpa and Grandma Cook's farm, and the Indian lady was standing by Grandpa Cook's barn.

"It was like she was trying to tell me something, but I'm not sure what."

"You can say that again," whispered Griffen. "We haven't been to the farm since last fall. I don't think we'll be going to visit anytime soon since Mom's leaving for Florida."

"I know. I just thought I would tell you what happened in the dream. You said the next time I had one you wanted to know."

"I don't understand all of this and right now I don't want to. We'd better get some sleep," said Griffen, as he crawled back into bed.

"Can I sleep in here with you?" asked Zeke. "I don't want to sleep in my room."

"Sure," replied Griffen. "My sleeping bag is right over there." Griffen pointed to the far corner of the room by his closet. He reached over and grabbed one of his pillows and threw it at his brother. Zeke caught the pillow, then crawled over and grabbed the sleeping bag.

Once Zeke had the sleeping bag spread out on the floor, he turned off the bedroom light. Lying down, he thought about the white light in his room, his dream, and his brother hearing a voice. He really wanted to understand what was happening. What was clear was that neither of them understood any of it. "You know Griffen, I really think we should tell Dad and Mom about what has been going on. It's too weird. What if it isn't safe?"

"No! Absolutely not! Either they won't believe us or they'll think we're crazy. Who's going to believe that a stick made a glowing white light in your room? Worse yet, who's going to believe that I hear voices?" Griffen chuckled, "Really, a voice that tells me not to be afraid and yet I have no idea where it's coming from? You don't hear it, only I do. Besides, then Dad will know that we snuck out of the campsite and went to the cemetery, when we both know we shouldn't have. I wish we had never gone to the cemetery because then none of this would be happening."

"Yeah, you're right. I won't tell them. I honestly can't believe it myself. There's no way anyone is going to believe us." Shaking his head in disbelief Zeke turned to lie on his side. Quietly he whispered, "Night, Bro. I would say sweet dreams, but I don't want you to dream what I've been dreaming about. It has to be scary enough hearing voices when you're awake."

Chapter 6

GRIFFEN AWOKE FIRST. THE MORNING sun shone brightly on his face and directly into his eyes. Pulling the blanket up over his head, he turned over to block the sun and started to drift back asleep. Hearing a light tap on his door, he called out, "Yeah?"

He heard the door open. Slowly, he removed the blanket from his face and turned toward the door. His mom stood in the doorway.

"Ah, I see you have a visitor in your room." Mom smiled as she saw her youngest son lying on top of the sleeping bag. "I have breakfast going. It'll be ready in about ten minutes."

"Okay, Mom," responded Griffen. "I'll wake Zeke up and we'll be right down."

"Thank you," said Mom, as she left the room.

Griffen let out a big yawn and got out of bed. Stepping over his brother, he went to the closet to find something to change in to. He quickly grabbed blue and white plaid shorts and a tank top. He really didn't care much about what he wore, except when he had to. Stepping back over his brother, he made his way over to the dresser to get some clean underwear and socks.

Noticing that his brother was still asleep, Griffen quickly thought of something that would wake him up. All he had to do was lightly place the end of his tank top on Zeke's face and move it slowly across his cheek. He had done this before and knew that it tickled when it was done right. It was funny to watch him bat it away with his hand. Instead, he took his foot and placed it on the top of his brother's shoulder and started shaking him back and forth.

"Wake up, Zeke!" He waited for a response. When Zeke didn't move, he did it again. After the third time, he got the reaction he was looking for.

"Stop it," snapped Zeke. "Leave me alone! Let me sleep!"

Griffen pretended not to hear him and shook him again. Yes, there were times it truly was fun to be the older brother. "You need to get up. Mom's cooking breakfast."

"I'm not hungry. Go without me."

"No, get up! Mom wants us both at breakfast today. She's leaving soon, remember?"

"Boys, breakfast is ready!" shouted Mom from the bottom of the stairs. "Get a move on, before it gets cold."

"Be right there, Mom!" returned Griffen.

Once again, Griffen used his foot to shake his brother. "You'd better get up."

"Okay, okay, I'm awake." Zeke sat up and watched his brother put on his tank top and then leave the room. Slowly he forced himself to get up and shuffle to his bedroom to change his clothes. He was almost there when he heard Mom call for them again.

"Be there in just a sec!" hollered Zeke. He quickly grabbed jean shorts and a red t-shirt, changed clothes, and headed downstairs for breakfast. As he bounded down the stairs, he could smell pancakes – his favorite! He knew that Mom had made them especially for him and Griffen. It would probably be awhile before they had them again since Dad was not a very good cook.

Zeke joined his brother at the kitchen counter. Griffen had already poured some warm maple syrup over his buttered pancakes. Just seeing it made Zeke's mouth water. He didn't have long to wait, because as soon as he sat down Mom placed a plate in front of him. He reached for the butter, cut off a big slab, and placed it in the middle of the pancake stack. Using his knife he moved the melting butter over the top pancake. He reached for the syrup and watched as it flowed over the top until it was dripping down the sides. Without any further hesitation, he cut a big hole in the middle of the stack and took his first bite.

"You're both moving pretty slow this morning," remarked Mom. "You still tired from your camping trip?"

"Not really," responded Griffen.

Suddenly, Zeke wanted to tell his mom everything about what had been happening. He knew if he did that his brother would be really angry with him, but that didn't matter to him. He knew he would tell her, just as soon as he finished chewing the food in his mouth.

"So tell me about this cemetery you visited. Your dad said that it was really old, and that you read some of the tombstones. Was it scary for you?" Mom didn't think that it had been a good idea to take the boys to the cemetery.

Carefully avoiding Griffen's eyes, Zeke said, "Yeah, Mom, I was a little scared. There was this tombstone that was taller than all the rest of the tombstones. The strangest thing happened."

Zeke ignored the kick that Griffen gave him under the counter and continued to tell his mom about seeing different words on the grave marker than what Dad and Griffen had seen. He also told her about bringing home a willow stick and putting it under his pillow.

Griffen decided to let him ramble on. He could tell that Zeke was bursting with the need to share the experiences with someone else. He even debated on whether or not he should tell Mom about the voice he heard. As it turned out, he really didn't need to debate.

Once Zeke started talking, it was like someone had turned on a faucet. He just kept going. He told Mom about Griffen hearing a voice that told him to also take home a willow stick and put it under his pillow.

"Ah, okay. Now I understand why the two of you were carrying those sticks to your room. When I asked your father, he said that you had wanted a souvenir from your visit." She laughed. "Well, I guess they would be souvenirs. So, you each got a willow stick and brought it home. Did you place them under your pillows?"

Excited that Mom was listening, Zeke bobbed his head up and down as he popped another bite of pancake into his mouth.

Glancing at Griffen, she asked. "And you? Did you put the willow stick under your pillow?"

Griffen just shook his head no.

Mom knew that her youngest son had a great imagination. She nodded as she listened. Thinking that he was done with his story, she smiled at both of her sons. "Well, I'm glad it wasn't too scary for you, and that you didn't see any ghosts."

"But I did, Mom!" piped up Zeke. "I saw an Indian lady by the entrance of the cemetery as we were leaving."

Zeke's dad glanced up sharply at him. This was the first he was hearing of this.

"Was it the same Indian lady that's been appearing in your dreams?" quizzed Mom.

"Exactly like her, Mom. I think it was her," answered Zeke eagerly.

Mom once again nodded her head, "Maybe she followed you there?"

"I don't think so," answered Zeke. He hesitated and then put another fork full of pancake into his mouth.

Zeke's mother gave him a long look. He looked like he had wanted to say something else, but she decided to let it go.

"Well, I don't want to change the subject, but I need you two to hurry up and finish eating. I need your help today," she said.

"With packing?" asked Zeke with a full mouth.

Mom tilted her head towards her son and pointed to his mouth. "Please don't talk with your mouth full." Zeke quickly closed his mouth and continued chewing.

"What do you need help with, Mom?" asked Griffen.

"I'll handle the packing. I need your help cleaning out the garage. I'm not sure how long I will be gone, and I want to make sure the garage is cleaned out this summer. You only need to handle your stuff. Put everything back where it belongs and sweep the floor."

Griffen felt his phone vibrating and reached into his pocket to retrieve it. It was Bugz. Bugz was short for Billy Underwood. He wasn't sure what the "g" and "z" stood for. Ever since he and Billy had gotten their phones, this was how he was identified. Most of his friends, at least his true friends that knew him well, referred to Billy as Bugz. Griffen read the message, "Meet me at the park."

Griffen texted back, "What time?"

"2"

"Mom, Bugz wants me to meet him at the park at 2:00 p.m. Can I go?"

"You can leave as soon as you finish the garage."

Griffen typed the following message on his phone, "c u there", and then put the phone back into his pocket. He grabbed his plate and took it to the kitchen sink. "I'm heading to the garage to get started." He leaned over and gave his mom a quick kiss on the cheek.

Mom quickly turned her head and gave him a kiss back. She had her hands in the dishwater or she would have also given him a hug. "One more thing, Griffen, I need you to be home in time for dinner tonight. We're eating at 6:00 sharp and I want us to have dinner together."

"Okay, Mom," answered Griffen. As he started out the door he yelled back over his shoulder to his brother, "Hurry up! I'm not cleaning the garage by myself!"

Zeke hollered back, "Be right there." He picked up his plate and took it to the sink. "Breakfast was great, Mom. Thank you!"

"Glad you enjoyed it. Zeke, thank you for admitting that you were a little scared at the cemetery. I know it's important for young men to feel brave. I think you were brave for just going there. I hope your Indian lady ghost friend doesn't bug you too much."

Zeke smiled. That's what he loved about his mom. He could tell her anything and she never made him feel bad about it. "I've got more to tell you, Mom, but I'd better go help Griffen right now. You know he'll get upset if I don't."

Journey with Zeke

"I think you're right," replied Mom, as she wiped her hands on a dish towel. She reached out and gave her son a big hug and a kiss on the cheek. She sure was going to miss them while she was away. "I'll be out in just a minute."

Standing in the middle of the garage, Griffen inspected the task at hand. "Boy, Mom is right! This garage is a mess."

"Where do we start?" asked Zeke.

"You're asking me?" replied Griffen. Both stood there for a few minutes taking in all the junk lying on the floor and on the garage bench. "Well," said Griffen, "I guess we can begin by putting all the sports equipment back into the totes."

Both boys quickly gathered the baseball gloves, bats, and baseballs, putting them back where they belonged. Next they put away the basketball, the football, and the skateboards. It took them over an hour to sort their stuff and store it correctly.

"Where's Mom?" asked Zeke. "I thought she was coming out here with us."

"I heard the phone ring a few minutes ago. When she answered I heard her say, 'Hi Mom.' She must be talking with Grandma B," responded Griffen.

"I hope Grandma is going to be okay," said Zeke.

"Me, too," replied Griffen. He was trying to be strong for his little brother. He didn't want him to know that he was really worried. Actually he was more worried now than the first time Grandma had been diagnosed with cancer. He remembered clearly how sick Grandma B had been, and he remembered the feeling when he saw his mom cry. Crying was something that their mom did not do often, so he knew that she, too, had been really worried. Even though he hadn't seen his mom cry this time, he was sure that she had.

"Wow, boys, you did a great job!" Mom stood in the doorway looking around at the garage. "I can't believe you got it all picked up so quickly. Now your dad will be able to park his truck in the garage again." Everyone laughed.

"Yeah," said Zeke, laughing, "He won't have to dodge balls anymore. Get it, dodge-balls, Dodgeballs?"

Griffen groaned. "Hey, Mom," said Griffen, "Was that Grandma B on the phone?"

"Yes, it was."

"How is she doing?"

Mom stood quietly for a few seconds. She searched for the right response. "She's doing okay," she finally replied thoughtfully. "She's excited that I'm coming and wishes all of you were coming with me. But she understands that's not possible right now."

"So, what time are you leaving tomorrow, Mom?" asked Zeke.

"My flight leaves at 9:30 a.m. I have to be at the airport by 7:30. You boys are welcome to come with your dad and me to the airport. That is, if you think you can peel yourself out of bed that early tomorrow morning." She started laughing again and so did the boys.

"I want to go," exclaimed Griffen.

"I just need to remember to set my alarm clock," chimed Zeke.

"I'll remind you," said Mom. "I just need one more favor and then the rest of the day is yours, until dinner at 6:00 p.m.," said Mom. "Would you please go to the backyard, pull the cushions from the chairs, and bring them into the garage?" Pointing to a now open space on the shelf she continued, "You can stack them right there." Once again, both boys agreed to help out.

Griffen and Zeke immediately left the garage and started walking toward the backyard. They had just rounded the garage when Zeke said, "After I went back to sleep last night, I had another dream about the Indian lady and the white wolf."

Griffen stopped and firmly grasped his brother's arm. He wanted Zeke to listen very carefully to what he had to say. "We have got to stop this. Do you understand? First, we visit a cemetery. You see strange things and I hear strange things. Then we bring home these stupid willow sticks. Your room lights up like a Christmas tree and mine makes me hear things again.

I don't know what is going on, and I really don't want to know. I just want all of this to stop. It's too weird and we need to focus on Grandma B!"

Zeke stood perfectly still. He was surprised at his brother's outburst. He felt tears well up in his eyes. He fought to hold them back and replied, "Don't get mad at me! I didn't ask for all this strange stuff to happen either. You were the one who said you wanted me to tell you when I had a dream. So here I am trying to tell you, but instead of listening to me, you're yelling that you want it all to stop!"

Griffen let go of his brother's arm. He felt cruel for making his brother cry. He knew Zeke felt just as stressed about everything that was happening.

"You're right," he said. "I don't know. I just feel like…I don't even know what I feel right now. I'm sorry! I do want you to tell me about your dreams. I think it's because of Mom going away, Grandma being sick, and all the other crazy stuff.

Zeke took a deep breath and looked down at the ground. "Are you sure?" he asked.

"Yes, everything's going to be okay. I do want to hear about your dreams, even if they are a little crazy," replied his brother, as he smiled and tried to lighten the mood.

Reluctantly, Zeke went on, "The Indian lady and the white wolf were in my dream again. She told me that her name was Moon Willow and that the white wolf's name was Ralphina.

Griffen's jaw dropped. "Did you just say her name was Moon Willow?"

Zeke grinned, realizing that his brother had immediately made the connection between the name of the cemetery and the name of the Indian lady. "I know. Spooky isn't it."

"No," answered Griffen, as he felt goose bumps on his arms. "I would say it's darn right creepy! Griffen thought for a moment. "Maybe you dreamed that she said her name was Moon Willow because that was the name of the cemetery. You saw the name of the cemetery first, and then you dreamt that she told you her name. Get it?"

"Hmmm," replied Zeke thoughtfully. I guess that's possible, but what about Ralphina? I don't remember seeing that name anywhere. I'm pretty sure I would've remembered it."

"Anyway, listen to this," continued Zeke. "Somehow she knew that Mom was going to Grandma's house, and…"

Griffen interrupted, "How did she know that?"

Zeke shrugged his shoulders. "I don't know."

"Go on," said Griffen softly. "She knew about Mom and Grandma. What else did she say?"

Zeke took a deep breath and tried to remember the exact words the lady had spoken to him. He knew that if Griffen was creeped out because of the Moon Willow name, he was really going to flip out. "She said…all will be as it is meant to be." And not to worry about Grandma B, that we would see her again. Then she said we would have fun at Grandpa and Grandma Cook's farm."

A look of surprise crossed Griffen's face. "What? We're not going to Grandpa and Grandma Cooks. Mom is going to Grandma B's. What is she talking about? I think she has the wrong grandparents."

"You're doing it again," responded Zeke. "I can tell you're getting upset. I don't know what she's talking about. I'm just repeating what she told me."

"I don't want to talk about this anymore," said Griffen, as he abruptly turned toward the backyard. "Let's go get the cushions and put them in the garage, like Mom asked. Then I'm off to the park to meet up with Bugz and do some skateboarding."

Zeke knew their conversation had come to an end. Actually he was relieved. He was tired of talking about the Indian lady, fighting with his brother because of her and then trying to figure everything out. "Okay, can I go with you?"

"Nope," said Griffen. "I need some time alone."

Neither of them said another word as they carried the cushions to the garage. With the cushions put away, Griffen grabbed his skateboard and

Journey with Zeke

headed for the sidewalk. "See you later," he called back, as he jumped on his skateboard and headed for the park.

"Have fun, and tell Bugz I said hey!" yelled Zeke.

At first, Zeke wasn't sure what to do with himself. He was very tired after not getting much sleep the previous two nights. Yawning, he went back into the house and headed for his bedroom. Bounding up the stairs two at a time, he reached his room and lay down on his bed. He thought about playing the new X-Box game that his friend Justin had given him, but he was too tired. Instead, he decided to just relax for a few minutes. Within two minutes he was sound asleep.

Zeke knew the volcano was about to erupt. The earth was trembling and his whole body was shaking. He knew he had to get out of there. With a deep breath he took a big leap....and suddenly awoke to find his big brother shaking him.

Griffin gave one last hard shake and said, "Wake Up!"

Peeking through half-opened eyes, Zeke replied groggily, "What are you doing here?"

"What do you mean?" answered Griffen.

"I thought you were at the park."

"I was, but I'm home now. Remember, Mom said we were having dinner together tonight and I needed to be home before 6:00 pm. It's five to six, so here I am."

"Did you have a good time?"

"We sure did! I performed my first *Ollie* today."

"Wow," said Zeke. "Isn't that where you slam on the back of the skateboard, jump up, and then land back down on the board?"

"Something like that," replied Griffen. "Come on, dinner's ready. Race you!"

Zeke jumped out of bed and raced his brother to the kitchen. When they entered the kitchen, Dad glared at them. How many times had he asked them not to run through the house? He decided not to say anything this time. He had some big news and he wanted his sons to be in a good mood when he shared it with them. He waited as they filled their plates before he addressed them.

"Hey, boys, your mom and I have a surprise for you two." Anxiously the boys waited for him to continue. "How would you like to go and stay for a week at Grandpa and Grandma Cook's?"

The brothers looked at each other, dumbfounded. Even though neither one of them said it out loud, they were both thinking the same thing. Zeke's dream had been right. Moon Willow, the Indian lady, had said that they would be going to Grandpa and Grandma Cook's. Now it was coming true.

Both the boys recovered enough to smile and respond with enthusiasm.

Griffen was the first to reply. "Cool! It's always fun to go to Grandpa and Grandma's farm." He loved the animals and swimming in the creek. Last time they visited, Grandpa even let him drive the tractor.

"When, Dad? When are we going?" asked Zeke.

"Tomorrow," Dad answered. I got a call this morning and have to go out of town on business, and your grandparents said they would be happy to have you stay with them for the week.

"But we have to take Mom to the airport."

"You're right, son. We'll take Mom to the airport bright and early tomorrow morning. After Mom's plane takes off, we'll drive to the farm directly from the airport."

"That doesn't seem fair. She'll miss out," offered Zeke in a quiet voice.

"It's all right, Zeke, I want you to go." His mother looked at all of them. She repeated it again. "I want you to go to the farm. I want you to relax, have fun, and play and play and play until you're so tired that you can't play anymore."

"Play at Grandpa's?" chimed in Griffen. "You know Grandpa. We'll have plenty of chores to do." Everyone laughed. Griffen was right. Grandpa Cook was all about teaching his grandchildren from a young age that you had to earn your way in the world. He was quick to teach them the value in doing a job right, but he also knew how to have fun. He had taken the boys hunting and fishing. They had even gone to a rodeo.

"After dinner I want you boys to get packed," said Mom.

That was that. They were going to the farm. Just like Zeke's Indian lady had said.

After dinner Griffen and Zeke headed to their bedroom to pack. "What are you packing?" asked Zeke.

"The usual," answered Griffen, "jeans, t-shirts, sweatshirts, my baseball cap, socks."

"Me, too," chirped Zeke, and then quickly added, "are you going to bring your willow stick?" Suddenly, he felt the mood change and his brother became really serious. Zeke wasn't sure if he should say anything more, or if he should just turn and walk away. Not wanting to get into another fight with his brother, he decided to just leave. He turned and started for his bedroom.

As he reached the door he heard Griffen announce, "Yes, I'm going to take my willow stick." Zeke smiled from ear to ear. For a split second he thought of running back to his brother to give him a big hug. "Better not", he thought to himself. Just leave it alone!

Griffen continued, "I have to admit I was really surprised tonight when Dad told us we were going to the farm. It was the last thing I expected with everything that was going on with Mom and Grandma B. You know what, Zeke? I believe you. I think we will see Grandma B again. I know it in my heart."

"Yep, Moon Willow said so," responded Zeke. "I don't really know who she is or why I dream about her, but for some reason I feel like I should trust her. I think you should, too. I like her a lot better now that she's talking to me."

Now that they were on the same page with their feelings, Zeke walked up to his brother and gave him a hug.

Griffen returned the hug and then snickered, "Get out of my room!"

Chapter 7

THE NEXT MORNING WAS HECTIC at the Cook residence. Mom prepared for Florida, the boys discussed Grandpa and Grandma Cook's farm, and Dad made final arrangements for his business trip. Even though everyone had packed the night before, there was the last minute stuff that they still had to gather, like shampoo, a toothbrush, and toothpaste.

Mom had to be at the airport by 7:30 a.m. for her flight two hours later. She knew she was pushing it, but she wanted the family to have breakfast together. Everyone had agreed and had set their alarm clock for an hour earlier than they had originally planned.

Zeke grabbed his duffle bag off of the floor of his bedroom. After completing a last minute check, he was about to head out the door when he remembered his pillow. Grabbing it, he uncovered the willow stick beneath it. He couldn't believe he had almost forgotten it. He picked it up and stuffed it in his duffle bag. Now he was ready. With his duffle bag, pillow and willow stick safely tucked away, he flipped off the bedroom light and headed for the kitchen.

As he passed Griffen's room, he noticed that the room was dark. Just to make sure that Griffen was awake he reached inside the door and turned on the light. Griffen was not in his room. He must have gone downstairs already. Zeke glanced over at his bed and saw that he, too, had grabbed his pillow. Zeke wondered if he also packed his willow stick because he didn't see it on the sheets. He turned off the light and headed downstairs.

The kitchen was buzzing with laughter. Even though they felt excited, there was sadness also. Mom's eyes were puffy. Zeke wondered if she had been crying. He sat down on a stool at the kitchen counter. She continued drinking coffee as she stood in her usual spot on the other side of the counter.

"Morning, Zeke," said Mom, as she walked around and gave him a hug. "Breakfast is on the stove."

"Thanks," said Zeke, as he jumped down from the stool to get himself a plate full of his mom's breakfast casserole. Dad and Griffen also filled their plates. Everyone sat at the table and talked excitedly about their plans. They also discussed when they would contact each other later that day to make sure everyone was safe and where they were supposed to be.

Looking at the clock, Dad said, "Okay, family, we better get on the road now if we want to get Mom to the airport on time. Load the dishwasher." Ten minutes later they were on their way to the airport.

At the airport, Dad helped Mom get her luggage to the check-in counter. It was a tearful good-bye, filled with hugs and kisses. The boys wondered when they would see her again. They watched as she went through the security checkpoint and turned around to blow them a kiss. They gave a final goodbye wave and headed to the car to begin their journey to the farm.

It was close to noon when they turned down the farm's long driveway. As they approached the large white house with its huge front porch, they could see Grandma Cook sitting on the porch swing.

Dad honked the horn to announce their arrival. He watched his mom raise her hand to wave at them. Dad stopped the truck near the front steps. Zeke was the first one out of the truck. He ran to the front porch, where Grandma stood waiting for them. She greeted him with a big hug. Hugs followed for Griffen and Dad.

"How was the drive?" asked Grandma.

"It went smoothly. The boys slept most of the way. I relaxed and listened to the radio," answered Dad. "It's so beautiful out here. I always enjoy the drive. You know, Mom, sometimes I really miss home."

Grandma nodded her head in agreement. "It's the country living you miss, son. It certainly is a different lifestyle than living in the city." Grandma patted her son on the back. "It's time for lunch." Turning to face her grandsons she asked, "You want some help with your luggage, or do you want to bring it in after we eat?"

"We'll get it, Grandma," responded the boys. They jumped off the front porch and went to the truck to get their luggage.

Dad held the door open for his Mother. They were standing in the living room when the boys entered with their luggage. "Go ahead and take your stuff to the bedroom. You know where to go." The boys had stayed with their grandparents many times and knew the way well. Griffen and Zeke proceeded up the stairs.

It was a big, two-story farmhouse. Three bedrooms were located upstairs. The boys had always shared a room when they came to stay. They were certainly old enough to sleep in their own room, but it had come to be tradition that they both slept in the same room.

When they reached the last door on the left, they opened it and entered a room with two twin beds, a dresser and a small closet. They tossed their duffle bags on the floor by their respective beds and then headed back downstairs for lunch.

Meanwhile, Grandma and Dad had gone to the kitchen to set the table. "Have a seat, Jack. I'm going to let your dad know that you all have arrived. But before I do, I wanted to tell you how sorry I was to hear about Pat's mom. I've been keeping her in my prayers."

"Thanks, Mom. Pat and I appreciate it. Pat left on the 9:30 a.m. flight, so she's already landed in Florida. I told her not to worry about calling when she landed because I know the cell phone reception out here isn't that great. I'll call her later."

"It's a lot better now, son," replied his mom. "They just installed a new tower down the road a bit."

"That's good to know. The boys will be excited. They brought their laptops and have become very reliant on their cell phones. They never leave the house without them. Sure is a lot different than when I grew up!"

"You can say that again. In my day, not only did we not have cell phones or computers, but we didn't have a TV either. In fact, we shared a telephone party line which meant five or six houses shared the same

Journey with Zeke

phone line." She laughed as she recalled the memory of listening to other people's conversations while they gossiped about each other. "If you were privileged you had what they called a 'private line', meaning no one else could hear your conversations and you could use the line anytime." Yes, times had certainly changed. Now phones were connected to peoples' hips and party lines were gone. Each person had a private line and they took it for granted. However, some things never changed. "Son, would you like the honors?"

Jack smiled, "I sure would, Mom." He headed out the back door. How many times had he done this in the past? Too many to count.

The boys had joined their Grandmother in the kitchen and heard the bell start ringing.

Out in the field, Grandpa lifted his head when he heard the bell. He didn't need a cell phone or a walkie-talkie. He liked doing some things the old fashioned way. When the bell rang, he knew that he was needed at the house. This had been their method of communication for over 40 years. It worked just as well today as it did 40 years ago. They still used the same old bell that his dad had used. He had applied a fresh coat of paint to it just last month, bright orange this time, making it easier to see it toward evening. He smiled as he walked to his mule. He had not seen his son, Jack, or his grandsons for eight months. The last time had been Christmas. He and Grandma had gone to visit their son and daughter-in law, Pat, for a week. It was hard living so far away. Grandpa lifted himself onto the mule and headed for the house.

Back at the kitchen, everyone made their own sandwiches. Grandma had set a plate filled with different kinds of lunch meat on the table, along with potato salad and homemade chocolate chip cookies. The back door slammed, just as the last sandwich was being made.

"Where are they?" Grandpa called out in a boisterous voice.

"We're in the kitchen, Grandpa," hollered Zeke.

Grandpa hugged his son and grandsons, telling each of them how happy he was to see them again. Then he walked around the table and planted a big kiss on Grandma's cheek. Blushing, she smiled, and told everyone to start eating.

Grandpa had just joined them at the table when they heard a dog barking. "Who's that?" asked Griffen, as he turned his head in the direction of the barking. "It doesn't sound like Jock."

Grandpa looked at Grandma and then back at his son and grandsons. "Well," he hesitated, "I'm sorry to have to tell you that Jock passed away a little bit ago."

The boys watched as Dad looked up from his plate with a surprised, hurt look on his face. "You didn't tell me that Jock had passed."

"I know, son," responded Grandpa, "I was going to call you, but then I got your call letting us know about Pat's mom. I didn't think it was a good time to tell you, so I didn't. I guess I should have. I'm sorry."

Dad paused as he considered Grandpa's feelings. He was hurt, too. "I understand," replied Dad, as he nodded and smiled at his father.

Griffen and Zeke were stunned. Jock had always been there when they visited, for as long as they could remember. Griffen spoke up, "I'm sorry, Grandpa and Grandma. I know that you loved Jock very much. I'll miss him."

"I'm sorry, too," added Zeke, glumly.

Grandpa moved in his chair. You could tell he felt a little uncomfortable. "Thank you, boys," he replied.

Grandpa pictured Jock in his mind, a beautiful German shepherd with brown and black markings. He had been a great companion for many years. Everyone could tell he was thinking about Jock from the look in his eyes. Finally, he spoke, "Jock would have been 16 years old on September 10th. He was a really good companion and we miss him a lot." Grandpa smiled and left the table. They all watched as he disappeared down the hall. Hearing the barking getting louder, they kept their eyes peeled. When Grandpa reappeared he had a blonde lab puppy in his arms. "Here he is," he said, as he sat the puppy on the floor.

The puppy was like a wind-up car that had just been released. He moved as fast as his traction on the floor would let him. Before they knew it, he was upon them. The pup reached Zeke first. He bent over to pick him up. The puppy squiggled with so much excitement that it was hard

Journey with Zeke

for Zeke to get a firm hold on him. "What's his name?" Zeke squealed with delight as he finally lifted the puppy into his arms.

"Barley," answered his grandpa. "We named him Barley, like the color of his coat."

The puppy started licking Zeke in the face. Zeke kept moving his head from side to side, but it didn't stop all the puppy "kisses". "I like the name Barley," said Zeke.

Griffen left his chair and went to pet Barley. "Can he sleep with us, Grandpa?"

"I don't see why not," he answered. Both boys smiled. "When you're done with lunch, you can take him outside to play, but you better be ready. He's a handful and has lots of energy to burn. I'm sure he will wear you both out."

"Sounds fun," responded Zeke, as he placed Barley down on the floor. "I can't wait." The boys quickly gulped down their lunch then asked to be excused so they could play outside with Barley.

"Take care of your dishes, and then you can go," answered Dad.

Grandpa and Grandma stayed in the house for the next hour visiting with Jack. It was always a good time catching up in person, instead of over the phone. Realizing that it was getting late, Jack told his parents that he needed to get on the road. He thanked them for watching the boys and assured them that he would be back before the weekend to pick them up.

Jack stood and headed for the front porch. His parents followed. He could see the boys playing with Barley and giggling. It brought back fond of memories of his visits and playing with Jock.

"Hey, boys," he called. "It's time for me to head home. Come give me a hug."

Both boys rushed to their dad, and each took a turn giving him a bear hug. "Behave for your grandparents, you hear me?"

"Yes, Dad!" they replied in unison. They were so excited about being at the farm and playing with the new puppy, Barley, that they barely noticed when Dad had driven away.

Lynette Teachout

Soon after their dad had left, Grandpa called the boys to the porch. "Come on, boys, we've got some chores to finish. I'm going to go get the mule and I'll meet you right back here. It'll be a lot faster than walking to the barn." Not really understanding the mule part, the boys sat down on the swing as their grandpa disappeared into the house.

Zeke pictured Grandpa's old four-legged mule and looked at Griffen. "How does he think a mule is going to be faster than us walking to the barn? There's no way all three of us could fit on it!"

"I don't know, maybe Grandpa's finally losing it."

"Don't say that! Grandpa's smarter than you are!" Zeke was quick to come to his grandfather's defense.

"Well you can ride the old mule, I'll walk!" Griffen shot back.

Hearing a noise coming from behind the house, the brothers stopped arguing.

"What is that noise?" questioned Zeke.

Griffen leaned over the railing of the front porch toward the noise. When he saw Grandpa round the corner on his "mule", he burst out laughing. "You're not going to believe this one, Bro."

Zeke jumped up from the swing to see what Griffen was talking about. A huge smile grew across his face as he watched his grandpa stop at the front steps.

"Hop on, boys, and grab Barley. He loves to ride! Old Bessie and I will get ya to the barn in a jiffy," exclaimed Grandpa.

The boys were thrilled with what they saw before them. Grandpa sat grinning in the driver's seat of his new John Deere all-terrain vehicle. Griffen gladly took the front seat next to Grandpa while Zeke and Barley sat in the back. "You sure are full of surprises!" yelled Griffen, as Grandpa hit the gas pedal and started for the barn.

Once they had arrived at the barn and Grandpa had turned "Old Bessie" off, the boys bombarded him with all kinds of questions, everything from when he got his new toy to why he named it "Old Bessie." If there was something that Grandpa was good at, it was telling a story with lots of humor. Old Bessie was the name of a mule his father, their great-grandfather, had owned. She had been his favorite mule and they had some good times together, except for the time when Old Bessie had bucked him off because a bee had slipped under her blanket. The boys laughed as they listened to Grandpa tell the story. When they had finally stopped laughing and joking around, they headed inside the barn.

Grandpa needed help re-stacking bales of straw that had fallen over. Plus, the next cutting would be happening soon and he needed to make room in the barn to store it. For the next thirty minutes they worked as a team restacking the straw bales.

"I think it's time for a break," announced Grandpa. "I'll be right back." He wasn't gone long. Upon his return, he handed each grandson a cold bottle of root beer. The boys gladly accepted. Working in the barn on a hot August day was stifling. Sweat drenched their clothes and ran down their foreheads.

Grandpa fetched himself a bale of straw to sit on. Once he was seated he opened his bottle of ice cold water and took a long drink. "Nothing like water to replenish the soul," said Grandpa with a chuckle.

"Speaking of soul, Grandpa, would it be okay to ask you how Jock died? I don't want to upset you, but I am curious," questioned Zeke.

"I'm not sure," answered Grandpa. "He went to sleep on his bed like he always did. The next morning when I called for him, he didn't come. I went to check on him, but he had passed away during the night. I guess his time was up."

"Did you cry?" asked Zeke.

"I sure did," replied Grandpa, as he stared out the barn door.

Griffen looked at his brother as if to say, "What gives; why all the questions?"

Zeke avoided looking at his brother. For some reason, he was curious about how Jock had died. He had a few more questions, so he kept prodding. "Do you think Jock went to heaven?"

Grandpa smiled. "I'm sure he did!"

"One more question, Grandpa, and then I'll quit," stated Zeke.

Grandpa picked up his water, took another drink, than replied, "Ask away." Grandpa wanted his grandsons to always feel comfortable coming to him about anything, and to know that he would listen and answer honestly. He also knew this would not be Zeke's last question.

"Okay," said Zeke. "You ready?"

Grandpa chuckled, "Ready."

"Do you believe in ghosts?" Suddenly Griffen understood why Zeke was asking so many questions. He rolled his eyes and started to interrupt, but stopped when Grandpa answered.

"That's an interesting question. I do remember one time, a long time ago. I was in the barn by myself. One of the horses was having a hard time giving birth and I was really worried. The vet was out of town, so I was on my own. If I remember correctly, it was around 3:00 a.m. Anyway, I looked up and for a split second, I swear I saw an Indian lady with a white wolf by her side, standing in the corner of the barn watching me. I can't be sure, because I was tired, and like I said I only saw them for a split second. You know, I had completely forgotten about that until just now."

Grandpa looked down at his feet, and then raised his head to look at Zeke. "I don't know whether or not this Indian lady was a ghost, but to answer your question, yes, I believe in ghosts."

"It was Moon Willow. I'm sure of it!" exclaimed Zeke.

"Moon who?" quizzed Grandpa.

Griffen couldn't stand it anymore. Zeke had said enough. Zeke would probably tell Grandpa about the willow sticks and how Griffen was hearing things. No, Griffen wasn't ready to admit that to his grandfather yet. He quickly jumped into the conversation, "Moon nobody. Zekey-Boy always thinks he has the answer, and he doesn't."

Grandpa could feel the sudden tension. Griffen was suddenly upset and didn't want to talk about ghosts. Maybe it frightened him? Not wanting to upset his grandson on their first day at the farm, he decided to let Griffen's comment go. Zeke decided to do the same. Barley simply sat wagging his tail and panting, oblivious to the drama.

"Let's get the rest of the bales stacked," suggested Grandpa. "It's almost dinner time and if we get this finished today, it's one less thing we need to do tomorrow." They all worked on the bales until their arms ached. Just when the last bale had been stacked, they heard a bell ringing in the distance.

"Come on, boys, you heard the bell. That means it's time for dinner." Grandpa stopped and closed the barn doors before he loaded himself onto Old Bessie. "Hold on tight, boys, here we go!"

When they had reached the house, Zeke let go of Barley. Barley jumped off the seat and headed straight for the back door. "Something smells really good," said Zeke, as he headed inside.

Inside the door, he saw Grandma carrying a plate of pork chops to the table. "Wow, Grandma, they smell delicious!"

"I bet you're both hungry. Get washed up, and by the time you're back I'll have everything on the table," proclaimed Grandma. The men headed to the downstairs bathroom to wash up. They noticed that Grandma had a clothes basket lying by the sink in the bathroom. Grandpa quickly took off his shirt, tossed it into the basket, washed up, and replaced his shirt with a clean white t-shirt. The boys followed suit, running upstairs to get clean t-shirts. Ten minutes later they sat at the table eating a dinner of pork chops, mashed potatoes, green beans and homemade biscuits.

"Did you get all the chores done?" asked Grandma.

"Yes, we did," answered Grandpa. "We're all ready for the new straw. The boys did a great job. I'm certainly happy they were here to help! It would have taken me a long time doing that job by myself."

Grandma reached over and patted Grandpa's hand, "I told you that I would help you."

"I know you did, and I appreciated your offer. If the grandsons had not been here to help me, I would have taken you up on it." Grandpa winked at Grandma as she went back to eating. "Anyway, hard work will make men out of them." He grinned at the boys, who smiled back. "We still have a couple hours of daylight left. How would you boys like to take the mini-bike for a spin after dinner?" offered Grandpa. "I think it's the least I can offer for all your help today."

The boys eagerly agreed. They were tired, but never too tired for fun. Riding the mini-bike was a rare treat for the city boys, even if they had to take turns.

After the boys finished eating, Grandma told them to leave their dishes and head outside to enjoy the rest of the daylight. Grandpa handed them the key and told them where they would find the mini-bike. As soon as they were out the backdoor, Griffen yelled, "Race ya!" The boys took off running towards the farthest barn from the house with Barley in hot pursuit.

Griffen reached the barn first. Zeke purposely lagged behind so he could make sure Barley kept up with them. When they had almost reached the barn, he bent over, scooped Barley up, and carried him the rest of the way. Griffen had already opened the barn door and gone inside by the time Zeke arrived. Placing Barley back on the ground, he entered the barn with the puppy trotting after him.

Sitting on the mini-bike, Griffen tried to start it. He could hear the motor wanting to fire. Griffen pushed down hard again to kick start the motor. This time, the motor sprang to life. Giving it a little more gas, Griffen used his feet to back the mini-bike out of the barn.

The boys spent the next couple of hours taking turns riding all over the farm. They noticed that the sun was starting to set, so they took the mini-bike back to the barn. Walking together back to the house with Barley following them, they saw Grandpa and Grandma sitting on the porch swing together.

"That was fun," said Zeke as he plopped down in a white wicker chair. At his feet, Barley sat on the gray porch floor next to him, panting, and wagging his tail.

"Looks like you've got a new friend," chuckled Grandpa. "I'm happy to hear that you both had some fun. Life is all about work and the rewards that go with it."

Grandma stood up. "You boys ready for a nice cold glass of homemade lemonade?"

"Sure!" they replied in unison. Grandma left the trio for a moment to get the lemonade. When she returned they continued to sit on the porch, sipping their lemonade and watching the sun set. It was so peaceful, as they listened to softly chirping birds, crickets, and tree frogs. The boys slowly sipped their lemonade until the ice cubes were all that remained.

Zeke was curious about what Grandpa was going to need help with the next day. He wondered if his arms would be able to move after the chores they had done earlier. "So, Gramps, what's on the agenda for tomorrow?"

Grandpa grinned. "Cleaning barns! That's always a fun job, don't ya think?"

Zeke sat back in his white wicker chair. "Are you saying that we'll be shoveling some really smelly stuff?"

"That's what I'm saying," replied Grandpa with a chuckle, then added, "Don't worry an hour into it and you won't smell it any longer."

"Really?" asked Zeke, as he plugged his nose.

"Really," answered Grandpa. "You'll need to get up at 5:00 a.m. Have you ever heard the saying, 'Early bird gets the worm?' "

Zeke shook his head, as he answered, "No, can't say that I have."

A few minutes later Griffen announced, "I'm going to bed. I can't keep my eyes open anymore." He stood and picked up his empty glass. "I'm not looking forward to waking up so early, and I'm already tired and sore, but I'll help. I can't imagine what I'll feel and smell like tomorrow when the chores are done!"

Zeke followed his brother's cue and excused himself, too. The boys gave both grandparents a good-night hug and headed upstairs to bed. Neither of them spoke as they once again changed their clothes. "See you in the morning, little bro," said Griffen kindly, as he turned over to face the wall.

Zeke turned off the light and flopped onto his bed. It squeaked a bit. "Night, Bro."

He thought about asking Griffen if he had brought his willow stick. "Oh, forget it. I'm not in the mood for an argument," he reflected. Zeke reached under his pillow and felt his own willow stick to make sure it was

Lynette Teachout

still there. Within a few minutes he heard Griffen snoring. "Boy, he must be tired," thought Zeke. "He never snores!"

A few minutes later Zeke suddenly remembered something that he had forgotten. Quietly getting out of bed so as not to wake Griffen, he went downstairs. Grandma was still awake and watching TV from the recliner. Quietly he asked her, "Where's Barley?"

She looked up and pointed to the other side of her chair. "I think you boys wore him out. He was so tired that Grandpa decided to let him sleep right where he was."

"Is it okay if I take him back to my room with me?"

"You'll have to get up with him if he has to potty during the night. Are you up to that?" asked Grandma.

"Yeah, I can do that," answered Zeke. Zeke picked Barley up and carried the tired pup back to his room. Both were sound asleep within a couple of minutes.

Chapter 8

"What is that noise?" Zeke groaned. "It is so annoying. Turn it off!"

Griffen found Zeke's reaction amusing. The noise had woken him, too. Realizing that the sound was coming from outside of the bedroom window, Griffen peeked out to investigate. He knew what he was looking for; he just needed to locate it. It took him a few minutes, but he eventually found the large, colorful rooster, sitting on top of a fence post. He watched and waited for the next "Cock-a-doodle-doo!" When he heard it, he smiled.

The sun was just beginning to appear above the far side of the corn field. It was beautiful and certainly something that you didn't get to see in the city. The corn field seemed to stretch for miles. It made him wonder how much land Grandpa owned, and how in the world he kept up with the farming.

Glancing over his shoulder, he saw Barley on the side of Zeke's bed, wagging his tail from side to side. Griffen went over and picked him up. "Bet you've got to go potty, don't you? Well, I do, too. I'll take you first, and then I'll go." He headed downstairs.

As soon as Griffen opened the back door he noticed the air was already muggy. It was going to be a hot day. As he watched Barley sniff the ground for just the right spot, Griffen spoke to him. "Yep, it's going to be one hot and muggy day, and guess what I have to do. That's right, me and my little brother get to shovel poop." The word that he really wanted to use began with an "s", but he knew that was a swear word. As much as he wanted to say it, he didn't, out of respect for his parents. They were strict on swear words.

Barley finished his business and quickly followed Griffen into the house and back upstairs. Zeke hadn't moved an inch since Griffen had left. He thought about not waking him just to see if he would get in trouble with Grandpa, but knew that then he risked having to shovel poop by himself. No way was he going to do that! Griffen reached over and grabbed his pillow. Raising it above his head he slammed the pillow across his brother's back.

"Stop it!" yelled Zeke.

"You've got ten minutes to be downstairs or Grandpa is coming up to get you." Griffen smiled to himself at his own humor. He didn't know if Grandpa was up yet, but he knew for sure that Zeke didn't know. He slammed the pillow down on Zeke one more time. This time he hit Zeke across his legs. When he didn't get a response, he put the pillow back on his bed and changed clothes. He made sure he wore the oldest clothes he could find. Tired of trying to wake his little brother, he left the bedroom.

Barley followed Griffen downstairs. When they reached the kitchen, he saw Grandma sitting at the kitchen table with a cup of coffee in her hand. "Is Grandpa up?" he asked.

"Oh, yes, dear. He's already outside gathering fresh eggs for breakfast." She took another sip of her hot coffee and sat the mug down on the table. "Guess I better let you out, shouldn't I?" said Grandma, as she looked at Barley.

"I already did, Grandma. I brought him down just a little bit ago, and then I went back upstairs to change my clothes."

"Thank you, Griffen. That was thoughtful of you. I wondered why he hadn't run for the door. He usually does. Actually, I thought maybe he had an accident in your bedroom and I was going to go looking for it."

Griffen smiled. "Don't worry, Grandma, I'll help with Barley."

She smiled back and asked, "Where's your brother?"

Griffen hesitated. Should he tell her the truth and say he was still sleeping, or should he lie and say that he was getting ready. Not wanting to get his brother into trouble, he simply said he would go check again to make sure he was awake.

Griffen bounded up the stairs, just like he did at home, two at a time. When he entered the bedroom, Zeke was sitting up in bed.

"Glad to see that you're awake. Grandpa's outside gathering eggs for breakfast. He's going to be back any minute, so you'd better hurry up." With that said, Griffen turned to leave the room.

"Hey, Bro," called out Zeke. "Don't leave yet. I have something to tell you."

"What?" huffed Griffen. He already had a good idea what it was going to be about. He really did want his brother to tell him about his dreams, but not every day and what seemed to be every minute. Maybe this time would be different?

"I had a dream last night," replied Zeke sleepily.

Griffen rolled his eyes. It was too early in the morning to listen to dream stuff. He wasn't in the mood. He snarled back, "I don't want to hear any dream stuff this morning."

"But it was about the Indian lady."

"I don't care who it was about! Just get dressed and come downstairs."

"Wow, what's got you so grumpy this morning?"

"What do you expect?" replied Griffen. "It's 5:30! Just give it a rest."

"Well, don't take it out on me! I wasn't the one who said we had to get up early!"

Griffen just shook his head and walked toward the door. As he left the room, Zeke heard him say, "I'm going to get some breakfast."

"I'll be right there," hollered Zeke. He heard his brother run down the stairs. Quickly changing his clothes, he ran downstairs to join the others in the kitchen. He kept thinking about his dream and how weird it was. He wanted someone to listen to him. If Griffen wouldn't, then he would tell Grandpa during breakfast.

Downstairs, Grandma had just cracked a couple of eggs into the frying pan. "How do you like your eggs, Griffen?"

"Hard, with the yolk done," answered Griffen.

"Same here, Grandma," said Zeke, as he entered the kitchen. She didn't need to ask Grandpa. She already knew that he liked his eggs sunny side up. He liked to soak burnt toast in the runny egg yolk.

"G'morning, Sunshine! Have a little trouble getting up this morning?" Grandma asked Zeke.

Zeke immediately looked at Griffen and made a face at him. Griffen started to make a face back, but noticed that Grandma was watching them. Instead he just smiled.

"Don't get upset with your brother, Zeke," scolded Grandma. "He didn't say a word. I think you owe your brother an apology for the face."

Zeke quickly apologized and then sat down in his chair and thought, "No fair. Why do I always get caught?"

The boys remained quiet as they sat at the table waiting for their fried eggs.

Hearing a noise coming from the living room and wondering if it was Barley, both of the boys looked to the doorway. In walked Grandpa. He was wearing an old pair of overalls, with a long sleeve, light weight, blue cotton shirt underneath.

"Hey, Gramps, I think you're going to get pretty hot today if you wear those clothes."

Grandpa laughed. "You think so? I don't figure that you two have on shorts, do you?"

"Uh, yeah," responded Griffen. "I've already been outside this morning and it's really muggy."

"Yes, it is," answered Grandpa, "but, I'm not sure that you would want to shovel manure in shorts. It's your choice, but I wouldn't recommend it."

The boys looked at each other and agreed that they would change into their old jeans as soon as they were done eating. Curious, Zeke wanted to ask why it was so important to wear jeans, but he would wait on that question. He had something much more important that he wanted to

Journey with Zeke

discuss with Grandpa. He was just about to bring it up when Grandpa asked Grandma if she needed any help.

"All set," answered Grandma. "The eggs are ready." She slid the eggs onto plates she had sitting by the stove, then carried the plates to the table. She had a basket of buttered toast, including a few burnt pieces, just for Grandpa. And she wasn't about to forget the homemade strawberry jam. She knew her grandsons loved jam. Hearing a timer go off, she went to the oven and pulled out the hot biscuits. It wasn't every day that she made biscuits, but her grandsons' visit was a special occasion. She wanted to spoil them, and this was one way she could do that.

Grandma Margaret had lived on a farm her entire life. If there was one thing she understood well, it was that the kitchen represented the heart of a home. It helped her keep everyone well fed and energized. Finally sitting down herself, she reached for a warm biscuit, applied a little butter, and added some strawberry jam. She enjoyed the food as much as everyone else.

Zeke cut up his eggs into little pieces. He liked putting some of the egg pieces onto his biscuit and eating them together. Feeling Barley at his feet, he broke off a little piece of the biscuit and slid it under the table. Barley eagerly took the food offering and then begged for more.

Grandpa saw what was happening. He asked Zeke not to feed Barley while at the table. He didn't want to form any bad habits. He explained the reason to Zeke, and then told Barley to go lie down. As young as Barley was, he was smart. He listened to Grandpa and stopped begging.

Watching Barley walk over toward the door and lie down reminded Zeke of Jock. That was where Jock had always lain. He looked at Grandpa and blurted, "I had a dream about Jock last night."

Griffen reacted immediately to his brother's announcement about his dream. Before anyone could respond to what Zeke had just said, Griffen yelled, "Shut up, Zeke!"

Startled by Griffen's sudden rude outburst, Grandma immediately responded, "Griffen, it is not respectful to tell your brother to shut up or to yell at him. You need to apologize."

Lynette Teachout

Embarrassed, Griffen looked over at his grandmother. "I'm sorry Grandma, but Zeke and his dreams are driving me nuts!"

"That may be true, but it still doesn't give you the right to yell at him. You don't need to apologize to me. You need to apologize to your brother."

Griffen grudgingly apologized to his brother, and then went back to eating his breakfast.

Grandpa studied both of his grandsons. He wasn't sure of the reason, but he knew there was tension between them. Deciding not to address his concerns at this moment, he directed his attention to Zeke. "Tell me more, Zeke."

Relieved and excited that his grandfather wanted to hear more, Zeke told him about how he had seen Jock sitting on the front porch in his dream. He was wagging his tail and he could tell that Jock was happy.

Grandpa reached over and touched his grandson on the shoulder. Zeke smiled. "Thank you, Zeke," said Grandpa. "It means a lot to me that you would share your dream with me. Now I know that Jock is in heaven and that he is happy."

Zeke looked at Griffen. Griffen glanced at him while he continued to finish the last of his breakfast. "Wow, Griffen," said Zeke. "They listen to me about my dreams. Maybe you should, too."

"You and your stupid dreams," responded Griffen. Griffen was still sore about being reprimanded by Grandma. She had no idea how often he had to hear Zeke go on about his dreams. He had tried to be patient, and yes, there were times that he actually wanted to listen. But now it was getting to be an every day occurrence, and it was extremely irritating.

Grandpa looked over at him. "Griffen," he replied, "Zeke's dreams are not stupid."

Griffen was quick to respond. "They are to me! I'm tired of hearing about them! You don't understand. I listen to him about his dreams all the time. Half the time they don't even make sense."

"I think you feel that way because you don't understand the dreams," responded Grandpa softly.

Journey with Zeke

"I know that," said Griffen, "but neither does Zeke. That doesn't stop him from going on and on and on…"

"No, I don't," exclaimed Zeke. "You've told me yourself that you want me to tell you about my dreams, but I don't think I will anymore!" He crossed his arms in a defensive position.

"Fine by me," snapped Griffen.

Grandpa and Grandma looked at each other. Grandma gave him a nod. Grandpa smiled at his wife. She knew what he was going to say, and they were both on the same page.

"I understand how you both feel," said Grandpa. "When I was a young boy, I, too, had dreams, just like you, Zeke."

Both boys looked surprised. Did they just hear what they thought they heard? With their curiosity peaked, both listened closely as their grandfather continued to explain.

"I tried to talk about my dreams with my parents, but they didn't want to hear about them because they could not understand them. I tried to talk with my friends, but they made fun of me. I felt alone for a long time. I learned not to talk about them, to just keep it inside." With a gentle smile on his face, he continued, "But that didn't stop the dreams. Some of them were scary. Some were funny. Some were sad, some were happy.

"One dream I remember clearly to this day was about my favorite horse. His name was Buster. I had raised him since the day he was born and spent every minute I could with him. I broke him myself so that I could ride him. Well, anyway, I had a dream that Buster was going to hurt his foot on a rock." Suddenly Grandpa went quiet and gazed off into the distance in remembrance.

Both brothers were fixated, waiting for the words to come. Finally, Zeke couldn't stand it any longer. He wanted to know what happened. "Grandpa, what happened?"

Grandpa had this far away look in his eye as he recalled the event. "I decided to tell my parents about my dream. I knew they didn't want to hear about it, but I didn't care. This dream really bothered me. So at breakfast, I told them that I'd dreamt that Buster was going to hurt his foot. We had just moved Buster to a new pasture. Dad told me to check the field for rocks, but I hadn't gotten around to it yet. Anyway, they both assured me that it was nothing to worry about. They told me to just let it go and not think about it, that nothing was going to happen to Buster's foot."

"I listened to them. Their response made me feel better. It was just a bad dream, or so I thought. Later that morning, my friend Austin came over and he wanted me to ride bikes with him. I asked my mother, and she said it was okay. So off I went. I was gone awhile, returning just in time for lunch. I remember clearly thinking again about my dream. I looked over at the pasture where Buster was feeding. Everything appeared fine, so I ignored this nagging feeling that I should go check for rocks. I figured I would do it after lunch."

"When I had finished up lunch, Dad asked me if I wanted to ride into town with him. I thought, sure, why not? Again I thought about my dream. I told myself that I would check for the rocks when I got home from town."

"We had just arrived home after being in town, when our neighbor Charlie stopped by for a visit. He had his dog, Skip, with him. Dad and I walked over to Charlie's truck to talk to him. At first, Charlie just sat in his truck and we talked through the open window. Dad had just gotten a new part for his tractor and was telling Charlie about it. He asked Charlie if he had a few minutes to help him put the part on the tractor. Charlie said yes, he would help him. Anyway, Charlie opened the truck door and started to get out. That was when I got this really strange feeling. I don't know that I can explain it, except to say it was quite an extraordinary feeling, as if things became crystal clear in my mind. You see, when Charlie opened his door to get out of his truck, Skip jumped out of the truck right behind him. Before Charlie could even say a word, Skip took off running toward the horse pasture."

"From that point on, everything happened fast. Buster saw Skip running toward him and didn't like the looks of it one bit. I remember hearing him neigh. I saw him shake his head and then he started galloping around the pasture."

"Charlie yelled at Skip to stop, but the dog just kept going. As soon as he reached the fence, Skip stopped, looked around, and trotted back to the truck. Buster, however, was still racing around the pasture. I heard him let out a loud whinny. That's when I noticed he was limping."

"I ran as fast as I could to him. I remember being so scared. As soon as I reached Buster, I grabbed his harness and started rubbing his neck to calm him down. I was so worried that I didn't realize that Dad and Charlie were right behind me."

"I looked at my dad and he looked at me. Charlie was apologizing. Once I got Buster calmed down, Dad lifted his leg and I could see blood on his foot. Looking around the pasture, I quickly spotted the rock that had caused the damage."

"I was so upset about what had just happened. I was instantly angry with Charlie and his dog Skip. I screamed at Charlie, 'Look what your stupid dog did to my horse! Look!'"

"Then I heard my father say very firmly, 'That's enough!'

My dad gently set Buster's hoof back on the ground. "It's going to be okay, son," he said. "It's not that bad. He has a little cut, but it will heal. We have medicine in the house. Why don't you go and get it?"

"I didn't want to leave Buster, but I did as my father told me. I ran to the house, quickly grabbed the medicine and within five minutes was back with them. Charlie kept apologizing but I was still so angry."

"Dad put the medicine on Buster's foot while I kept him calm. Once we all knew that Buster was going to be okay, we headed back to the house. Dad and Charlie were talking about something on the way back. I was in a bit of a daze and was only half listening. That's when I remembered my dream from the night before. I stopped in my tracks."

"Dad and Charlie took a couple more steps. Then they stopped and turned around to look at me. I heard my dad say, "You okay, son?" Wanting to reassure me he added, "Buster is going to be okay.""

"I stood there in silence for a moment recalling the details of the dream. Then it hit me. What happened was really my fault. I didn't know how to explain this to my Dad or Charlie. Instead, I walked up to Charlie and put my hand out in a peace offering."

Grandpa chuckled a little bit. "From the look on Charlie's face, I think I startled him. Charlie slowly reached out and shook my hand. At the same time, he apologized again. I smiled at him and told him not to worry about it. I shot a quick look over to my dad. He had a smile on his face. I knew without another word being said that he was proud of me. His smile told me everything."

"Wait a minute," interrupted Griffen. "I don't get it. Why would it be your fault, when it was Charlie's dog that scared your horse?"

Beaming, Zeke spoke up, "I get it, Grandpa. You had a dream that Buster was going to hurt his foot on a rock. You were supposed to go to his pasture and pick up any rocks you could find. Instead you did other stuff. You slacked off from your job. If you had picked up the rocks earlier, Skip still could have scared Buster, but he wouldn't have stepped on a rock and hurt his foot. The rocks wouldn't have been there."

"That's right, Zeke," answered Grandpa.

"Okay, let's just say that you're both right," quizzed Griffen. "I still don't understand about the dream. Was it a bad dream that came true, or was it a premonition, or whatever?"

"Great question, Griffen. Sometimes when we dream something and it appears to us to be a bad dream, it really isn't. Instead, I believe the dream is trying to tell us something, and we need to pay attention to what it's trying to tell us. In this case, my dream was telling me I needed to pay attention and remove the rocks from the pasture. The best way to describe my dream is to say it was a protection dream."

"So, if I have a dream that tells me that I should jump off a bridge, should I do it?" asked Griffen.

"No," replied his Grandpa. "You should never listen to a dream that tells you to do something bad to others, animals, or to yourself."

Griffen shrugged his shoulders. He really wanted to understand, but he couldn't wrap his mind around it all. He didn't want his brother or Grandpa to know that he was still confused, so instead of questioning any further he changed the subject. "Look what time it is. We better get our chores done. Don't you think, Grandpa?"

"Well, Lordy be! You're right, Griffen. I am already 20 minutes behind schedule. "Come on, boys, let's get to it."

The morning flew by. There had been no time to ask more questions about dreams, ghosts, or anything else for that matter. They fed the chickens, milked and fed the cows, and threw hay for the horses. Cleaning the stalls wasn't all that fun, but it needed to be done. And yes, even though it was hot out, they were glad they had worn jeans. It was just about noon when they heard the bell ringing.

"Did you hear the bell, Grandpa?" asked Zeke.

"I sure did. Let's head for the house and get some lunch."

Grandma was filling the last glass of lemonade when they entered the kitchen. "Hey boys, you need…" Before she could finish her sentence, Griffen jumped in, "We know, Grandma. We'll wash up first, and then I'm putting on some shorts."

"Me too," chimed in Zeke. "These pants smell pretty bad."

"Thank you," she replied.

Sitting down to a lunch of tuna fish sandwiches, potato salad and ice cold lemonade, Zeke wondered if it would be a good time to bring up his dream again. Grandpa had answered some of his questions, but had not answered why he had been the one to have the dream about Jock. He was curious as to why Grandpa hadn't had the dream. After all, Jock was his dog. Before he could ask the question, Griffen asked a question of his own.

"Grandpa, can Zeke and I go fishing this afternoon at Wilder Creek?"

"Sure, you boys worked hard this morning. I think you should relax a little this afternoon. You can take Old Bessie."

"Seriously, Grandpa, I get to drive Old Bessie?" exclaimed Griffen, not sure he had heard right.

Zeke wasn't about to let this opportunity get past him. "If you get to drive, Griffen, I want a turn, too!"

"I'll show you both how to start her up and how to drive her safely, right after we finish lunch. Griffen, you can drive to Wilder Creek, and then let Zeke drive home."

Zeke was so excited that he immediately jumped up from the table, grabbed his plate, silverware and glass, and headed for the sink. "I'll be ready in five minutes," he called out to everyone. "I just need to grab my fishing pole and gear from the bedroom. And, oh yeah…I need to change my clothes and get my swim trunks."

"I'm right behind you", said Griffen as he quickly picked up his lunch dishes and head to the sink. I'll meet you outside Grandpa in just a few minutes," yelled Griffen, as he followed Zeke up the stairs. Barley didn't know what was going on, but he was up on his feet wagging his tail. From the sound of the excited voices and the movement around the table, he knew they were going somewhere.

Grandpa waited for the boys in the air conditioned kitchen. Within a couple of minutes Griffen returned. Together they walked outside. Grandpa lifted Barley up and placed him on the front seat. Barley knew right where to sit. He had done this many times before. Griffen sat in the driver's seat. He watched and listened intently as Grandpa showed him how to start the ATV, how to make her go, and how to make her stop. "Go ahead and take Old Bessie for a spin," said Grandpa, as he pointed to the path around the house.

Griffen didn't need to be told twice. He placed his foot on the gas peddle and with both hands on the wheel, drove down the path. With the wind in his face, he made a quick trip around the house. When he returned, Zeke stood outside with all the fishing gear and poles. He pulled up and stopped. "All aboard!" he announced to his brother.

Zeke jumped on. "Hey, is Barley supposed to be going with us?"

"He's a good swimmer, but he's still young, so don't let him go out too far," answered Grandpa. "All you need to do is call his name and he'll come back. I have to get one more thing, boys. Stay right here. I'll be right back." Grandpa turned and hustled back into the house. The boys looked at each other, wondering what was going on. It wasn't long before Grandpa returned and handed a container to Zeke.

"Oh, yeah," said Zeke, sheepishly. "It does help to have bait when fishing." Grandpa nodded in agreement.

"Make sure you're back to the house by 5:00 p.m. Grandma is a very punctual person and I promise you we will be eating dinner by 5:15 p.m." Everyone laughed. They understood that when it came to eating, there was a schedule to follow. The boys gave a thumbs-up signal. "Let's go!" exclaimed Zeke.

Griffen slowly drove away. Once they were out of Grandpa's eye sight, however, Griffen pushed the gas pedal to the floor. He cared not about safety. The thought of getting hurt never even crossed his mind. He simply wanted to go as fast as possible. The resulting wind ruffled their hair. Even when they hit a bump and both he and his brother were bounced off the seat, he didn't slow down. This was fun! Barley bounced back and forth between them as Griffen turned the wheel from one side to the other. The brothers laughed out loud. Zeke screamed, "Do it again! Do it again!"

About twenty minutes later they had arrived at the creek. Griffen slammed on the brakes and jerked to a sudden halt. Zeke reached over and grabbed Barley to keep him from sliding off the seat. Griffen jumped out and ran around to the back. Reaching for his fishing pole, he heard his phone start ringing. He immediately recognized the ring tone.

"Hey, it's Mom," announced Griffen as he answered. "Hi, Mom!"

Zeke walked around the vehicle to stand next to his brother. "Put her on speaker so I can listen and talk, too!"

"Hang on, Mom. Let me put you on speaker." With a click both Griffen and Zeke were conversing with Mom.

"Hi, Guys. Are you having fun?"

"We're having a great time, Mom," responded Zeke.

Griffen confirmed, saying, "Yep, having fun."

Zeke asked her about Grandma B. There was a slight hesitation before they heard her say, "Grandma B is doing well. She will be starting her treatments soon. She sends her love to both of you, and so do I."

"Hey," she continued, "Dad will be back from his business trip by the end of the week. He said that he had just talked to Grandma and got a report that both of you have been really helping out with the chores. I heard you earned some relaxation time to go fishing."

"That's where we are right now, Mom," explained Zeke.

They heard Mom laugh. "Your dad also mentioned that Grandpa has a new puppy named Barley and something about Old Bessie. Not sure that I know who Old Bessie is!"

The boys laughed. "Oh, Old Bessie is a mule," said Griffen.

"You're riding a mule around?" The boys knew that their mom was picturing a four legged animal, just as they had. "Are you riding a mule around?" she asked again.

"You could say that, Mom," giggled Griffen. "A really fast and loud mule!" Both boys burst out with laughter.

"Well, be careful. I don't know anything about mules. I don't know how safe they are. For all I know you could be kicked or get bitten. I am going to trust Grandpa on this one. I know he would never do anything to put you in harm's way."

"We're safe, Mom," reassured Zeke as he giggled to himself. Kicked or bitten? No, it would be more like rolled on or thrown off!

"Okay, you boys be careful." You could hear the relief in her voice. "I need to go now and help Grandma B. Both of you listen to your grandparents and have a great time. Like I said before, Dad will be there by the weekend to pick you up. Oh, and before I forget, Dad lost his cell phone. You won't be hearing from him until he returns from his trip. If something comes up, just give me a call."

"Will do," responded Griffen. "Love you, and send our love to Grandma B."

Mom sent her love again to both sons. Griffen pressed the 'end' button and looked at his brother. "Let's go fishing and catch some dinner." The

Journey with Zeke

brothers picked up their fishing gear and hurried toward the creek. Barley followed close behind.

After fishing for half an hour without a single nibble, both brothers became bored. "I think it's time to go swimming", suggested Griffen. With that he let out a loud whistle. "Hey, Barley, want to go swimming?" Barley jumped up and started wagging his tail.

"Come on, boy!" exclaimed Zeke, tapping his hand against his leg as he started splashing into the creek.

Griffen found a large stick lying on the bank. He picked it up and threw it into the water. Hearing the splash as the stick hit the water; Barley quickly went to retrieve it. In the deeper part of the creek, he doggy-paddled quickly and held his head above the water. When he returned, he had the stick in his mouth. The brothers took turns throwing the stick for Barley. Grandpa was right. Barley was a good swimmer. Soon the boys joined Barley in the water. Together, they swam and played until they were too tired to swim anymore.

After the boys dried off with their towels and Barley had shaken the water off his body several times, the boys sat down to enjoy a snack. Zeke broke off a piece of his homemade peanut butter cookie and offered it to Barley. "What time is it?" asked Zeke. "You know we have to be back by five."

Griffin nodded and jumped up to get his phone. "It's 2:30," said Griffen. "Do you want to head back, or go for a ride on Old Bessie?"

"Neither," answered Zeke. "I'm pretty tired. I just want to sit here awhile under this tree and relax." Zeke enjoyed nature. He loved listening to the birds and the sound of the water, as well as the sound of leaves rustling in the breeze. Living where he did, he didn't often have the opportunity unless he went camping. He wanted to take advantage of this beautiful afternoon and enjoy his surroundings. It was a great way to relax.

"Okay, you keep Barley with you. I'm going to take Old Bessie for a spin down some of the trails."

Zeke thought for a moment before agreeing. Part of him wanted to go with Griffen, but he really was tired and really felt like relaxing. "Okay," answered Zeke, "have fun!"

Griffen jumped on the ATV and started her up. Zeke watched his brother until he disappeared over the hill. He could still hear the motor off in the distance and could tell that Griffen was driving pretty fast again. Feeling sleepy, he laid down on the soft grass under the shade tree to relax and watch the clouds. Barley watched Zeke as he lay down and plopped down beside him. It wasn't long before they were both sound asleep.

Chapter 9

ZEKE FELT HIS BODY FLOATING. It was awesome, feeling so weightless. At first he floated in and out of big, white, fluffy clouds. Suddenly the scenery changed and he found himself floating above the tops of huge trees. Everywhere he looked, all he could see was the color green.

He felt himself slowly descending. In a blink of an eye he was soaring below the tree tops and was following a river that seemed to disappear into the mountains. As he soared closer to mountain, he noticed an opening in the mountainside. Sure enough, he floated into the opening and out the other side. This time, when he looked down, he saw field upon field of orange poppies. The beauty was breathtaking. He turned his head to see how far the fields went. When he turned back he was floating over his grandparents' farm.

Off in the distance he could hear church bells ringing, and felt his body shift to float toward the sound. Suddenly he found himself standing in front of two huge, white, wooden doors. Sensing he was not alone, he looked around. He couldn't see anyone, but he sensed that someone was watching him. He opened the large doors to the church and entered. He instinctively knew this was where he was supposed to be – his destination.

Once inside, he recognized the church. He had been here before with his parents and grandparents for church service. It was a beautiful church. Each side was lined with beautiful stained glass art work. The long, wooden pews extended from the back of the church all the way to the front. On the back of each pew he saw a set of bibles.

Suddenly feeling a pull to look toward the pulpit at the front of the pews, he did. What he saw surprised him. It was a casket. The lid was open.

Looking around, he thought, "Shouldn't other people be here with me? Where is everyone? Why is there a casket with the lid open at the front of the church?" He moved closer. He could see that someone was lying in the casket, but he couldn't make out who it was.

He found it odd that he was in a church all by himself with a casket, and yet he didn't feel afraid. Not wanting to stare at the casket as he moved to the front of the church, he drew his eyes toward the floor. He noticed different colors of light reflected on the carpet. Looking up at the stained glass windows, he saw that when the sun beams hit the window, the church floor filled with colors of blue, yellow, red and green.

Zeke felt the urge to keep moving forward. Finally, the casket was only a few feet away. Lying in the casket was his grandpa. Zeke screamed, "Grandpa!" and started to reach for the casket. Yet, no matter how hard he tried to approach, the casket stayed the same distance away.

He could feel tears running down his face. Again he screamed, "Grandpa!" Slowly, the casket lid began to close. Trying even harder, he was determined to reach the casket. Again, he had no luck. It didn't matter what he tried to do or how hard he tried. Feeling totally frustrated he screamed, "No! No! No!"

Chapter 10

ZEKE AWOKE WITH A START and felt something wet running down his face. He was hot and there was a bright light penetrating his eyelids. Opening his eyes, he was immediately blinded by the sun and realized the wetness was a mixture of tears and beads of sweat. Moving his hand up, he wiped his eyes, then looked for Barley. He spotted him lying on the other side of the tree, where it was now shady. "Smart dog," thought Zeke, as he got up and moved over to him.

As he petted Barley, Zeke thought about his dream. How in the world could a dream go from being so peaceful to ending up being one of his worst nightmares?

Meanwhile, Griffen was enjoying his time alone exploring the trails through the woods. With the wind hitting his face, he sped along. After an hour he felt a vibration and then another. He stopped Old Bessie, reached into his pocket, and saw he had a text message from Zeke.

"Where r u? Come back."

Griffen was a master at texting. He hit the "k" key and then "Send." He wondered what his brother wanted. He hadn't been gone that long, had he? Looking at the time on his phone, he realized he had been gone for over an hour. He wondered if his brother was going to be upset with him. He quickly dismissed the thought. He had asked if he wanted to go with him and he had said no.

Within five minutes Griffen pulled up to his brother, who was standing a few feet away from the creek. Barley was by his side and happily greeted Griffen as he jumped off the ATV. "What's up?" Griffen said to his brother.

He could tell from the look on his brother's face that he was not happy. In fact, he looked like he had been crying. "Are you alright, Zeke?"

Zeke didn't know how to respond to the question. He had just awoken from a nightmare. He wanted to tell Griffen about it, but knew that his brother got extremely annoyed when he talked about his dreams. But this was not a dream he wanted to keep to himself.

"Griffen, I just had the scariest dream," stammered Zeke.

"Oh, here we go again," responded Griffen. He rolled his eyes. "You mean to tell me you called me back from having fun because you had a dream?"

Zeke didn't let his brother say another word. "Listen to me," he demanded. "I dreamt that Grandpa was in a casket at a church."

Startled, Griffen paused. Then instinctively he slowly reached out to comfort his brother. "Wow, Zeke, I'm sorry you dreamt that about Grandpa." Griffen could tell that his brother was really shaken by his dream, but he really didn't know what to say. "Just try and forget about it."

"No!" yelled Zeke, as he backed away from his brother. "I can't just forget about it. What if it was real somehow? We need to go back to the farm right now. I need to know that Grandpa is okay!" Zeke's eyes began to tear up.

"Fine," said Griffen, with a bit of frustration. "Let's load everything and head back."

The brothers quickly picked up their fishing gear and loaded everything onto Old Bessie. With Barley sitting between them, they headed back to the farm. Zeke was so upset about his dream that he forgot it was his turn to drive.

As soon as they reached the back door of the house and Old Bessie had come to a complete stop, Zeke jumped off and ran inside. He shouted for Grandpa as soon as he opened the back door.

Grandma stood in the kitchen when Zeke came busting through the door. She had been watching them drive up the lane. She had worried about Grandpa's decision to let the boys take Old Bessie by themselves.

Would they remember how to get to the creek? What would happen if the ATV broke down? "You worry too much," he had told her. He was right. She was a worrier.

She heard the panic in Zeke's voice. He yelled for Grandpa even louder the second time, as he moved from the kitchen to the living room. "Grandpa, where are you?"

Grandma immediately followed Zeke into the living room. "Zeke, what's wrong?"

Zeke had been so focused on finding his grandpa that he hadn't noticed his Grandma standing in the kitchen. Turning to face her, he said, "Where's Grandpa?"

"He went into town to get a haircut," she responded. "Is something wrong?"

"Is he okay?" stammered Zeke.

"I'm sure he is," she answered calmly. She had no idea what had Zeke so upset, but she could tell he was really shaken. She heard the back door slam. Glancing away from Zeke, she saw Griffen enter the kitchen with Barley. Immediately, she returned her attention to Zeke.

"Honey, what's this about? Why are you so upset? Did something happen?" She could see Zeke had tears in his eyes. While she waited patiently for him to respond, she quickly looked over his body. "No blood," she thought. Then she looked at Griffen and Barley and came to the same conclusion. "No blood." She told herself to remain calm and give him time to respond.

"What's Grandpa's cell phone number, Grandma? I need to call him!"

"Honey, Grandpa doesn't have a cell phone."

"So, there's no way to reach him?"

"Maybe I can help you until he gets home," she replied.

"No, Grandma. I need to talk to Grandpa right now and make sure that he's okay!"

Sensing the urgency and not getting an answer from Zeke, she looked over at Griffen. "What's this about?" she asked with concern.

Griffen did not want to get involved. He wasn't going to be the one to tell her that all of this was because Zeke had a dream. Shrugging his shoulders, he answered, "I don't know."

She turned back to Zeke. "You must tell me what this is about or I can't help you."

Grandma listened as Zeke told her the details of his dream. When he had finished, she marched right over to the kitchen phone. Zeke watched as she dialed a number. Then he heard her say, "Hi, Dan, this is Margaret. Is George still there?" In a few seconds, Grandma continued, "Hi Honey, I forgot to ask you to pick up some milk on the way home for dinner." Zeke relaxed as he listened. Grandma was looking at him with an understanding smile on her face. Grandpa must have asked her if there was anything else that he needed to pick up. Grandma said, "No, dear, that's it, just some milk."

Hanging up the phone, she motioned for Zeke and Griffen to sit down at the kitchen table. Quietly, they all pulled out a chair and sat down.

"I know that some dreams can be scary, especially when you don't understand the dream. Zeke, do you have a lot dreams like the one you did today?"

"No, not like the dream I had today about Grandpa. This is the first time," replied Zeke.

For the next twenty minutes, Griffen listened as Grandma and Zeke discussed dreams. She told them a story about when she was younger and she had a dream much like Zeke's. She had been afraid to tell anyone. Her dream had been about Clara, a close friend of hers.

A couple of weeks after she had the dream, she received a phone call from another friend letting her know that Clara had died in a car accident. The memory of her dream had come flooding back. Grandma paused, and the boys could tell that even though the event had happened several years earlier, it still had an impact on her. After pausing for a couple of moments, she shared something with them that she had never shared with anyone. "To this day I wonder if I could have prevented her accident.

Journey with Zeke

"I keep asking myself why I had that dream in the first place. I haven't had one like it since. Recently I watched a program, can't remember the name of it, but the show was about people who have had similar experiences." She reached out and put her hand over Zeke's hand.

"Anyway, what I took away from the program is that some people's dreams predict the future. Some people have these types of dreams all the time. Others may only have one their entire life, like me, and yet others have them only periodically."

"Here's the best advice I can give you both. Listen to your dreams and don't be afraid to talk about them, especially when you don't understand them. And remember that no matter what happens, if the dream comes true or doesn't come true, you can't carry any guilt with you."

Removing her hand from Zeke's, she smiled and stood up. "I think it's time for some cookies." As she left the table she debated how much more she should tell her grandsons. She had questions that had haunted her for years like, "What if I had said something to Clara? Would that have made her so nervous that it could have caused the accident to happen? Or, what if her friend had told someone else about the dream, and after the accident had happened, that other person would think that she had something to do with causing the accident?"

Deciding not to say anything further, she sat the cookies down on the table. After all, if she didn't understand it all, how could she explain it?

Just as they finished their cookies they heard a car door shut. Grandma smiled over at her grandsons. "Okay, I'm going to get dinner started. Why don't you two go see if Grandpa needs any help?" Zeke went around the table and gave Grandma a hug.

"Grandma, can I ask you one more question?"

"Sure," she responded.

"Should I tell Grandpa about my dream?"

"Honey, that's up to you. You do what you heart tells you to do."

Zeke smiled. "Maybe I'll tell him later. Right now, all that matters is that he's okay."

Zeke ran outside to help his grandpa. He saw Griffen carrying the milk as they headed toward the house. He met them half-way and gave Grandpa a tight hug.

Grandpa chuckled. "Wow, guess I better let you two go fishing every day! So tell me, did you catch a lot of fish today?"

Griffen and Zeke looked at each and laughed. "No," answered Griffen. "We didn't get a nibble. But we did have fun swimming and driving Old Bessie."

"And what about you, Zeke, did you like driving?" quizzed his grandpa.

Zeke looked over at Griffen and replied, "I decided to wait until tomorrow to try driving."

Grandpa nodded at Zeke and then moved on to another subject. "Boys, before I forget, your dad called from work today. He wanted to let you boys know that he lost his cell phone, so that's why you haven't heard from him. He said to tell you that he'll be here to pick you up on Friday."

"Oh, we already know. Mom called us earlier," said Griffen.

"Oh, is that right?" responded Grandpa. Chuckling, he leaned forward and whispered just loud enough for the boys to have to pay attention. "Well, I have some news that I know you haven't heard yet."

"Really, what is it?" asked Zeke.

"I let your dad know that I'm going to take you camping and fishing for a couple of days. From what I hear, you two are pros at setting up your tent, gathering firewood, and telling some good ghost stories. The neighbor boys are going to handle the chores while we're gone. We'll be leaving in the morning."

Griffen grinned, "So no more shoveling poop?"

"Nope," replied Grandpa. "I want to spend some quality time with my grandsons. I don't want you to think that every time you come to visit it's chores, chores, chores. Yet, I did appreciate your help, and both of you were good workers. I just think it's time for some fun. If we hurry we can have everything packed and ready to go before dinner so we can head out first thing in the morning." Everyone agreed.

After dinner the trio departed to the barn's "Man Cave" to watch a movie. Grandpa had built the room long before anyone ever came up with the name. It was his special place where he could go to have some alone time or converse with other farmers who enjoyed watching sports or playing cards. Yep, every farmer for miles around knew about Grandpa's "Man Cave." It was nothing really fancy, but it had everything they wanted for relaxation, including a big screen TV.

During the movie, Zeke pondered on whether or not this was a good time to tell Grandpa about his dream. Every time he thought about it, he chickened out. He couldn't figure out a good way to tell Grandpa that he had seen him lying in a casket. Plus, Griffen was there. He really wanted to tell Grandpa when he was by himself.

Throughout the movie they all fought to stay awake. They'd had a long day, getting up at the crack of dawn, doing chores in the morning, playing in the afternoon, and then packing for their camping trip. Even though it was only 8:00 p.m., they decided it was time for bed.

Everyone said their good-nights. Griffen stayed behind to drink a glass of milk and then went upstairs himself. When he entered the room, he heard his brother snoring and saw that Barley was already asleep, curled up on the foot of Zeke's bed. After changing his clothes, Griffen climbed into bed. Even though he was really tired, he still felt exhilarated. Reflecting back over the day, he had to admit that being at the farm was hard work, but it was also lots of fun. Trying to imagine what it would be like to live on a farm full time, he quietly drifted to sleep.

Chapter 11

ZEKE FOUND HIMSELF STANDING INSIDE the same church that he had been in before. He didn't float this time; he was just there, standing in the back. Everything else was the same: the pews, the bibles, the stained glass windows, and the casket.

He looked around to make sure he was the only person in the church. He had been alone in his last dream, and since everything was so familiar, he figured he was alone once again.

Just like last time, when he tried to move closer to the casket, he couldn't. It was as if there was an invisible shield that would only allow him to get within six feet. That distance didn't let him touch the casket to make sure it was real. He really wanted to know for sure that the person that looked like his grandpa was indeed Grandpa.

Suddenly, a white mist appeared on the right side of the casket. He watched the mist take the form of the Indian lady, who floated next to the casket. He instinctively knew her name was Moon Willow. She always wore the same thing, a long, tan Indian dress. He wasn't sure if it was because of her long dress that he couldn't see any feet, or if it was because she didn't have any feet.

"Hi, Zeke," said Moon Willow.

Zeke heard her soft spoken, high pitched voice. He wanted to get closer to her, but just like with the casket, he couldn't. His feet were glued to one spot. There was something about her that struck him as funny. When she spoke, her mouth didn't move, but he could hear her speaking. "How is that possible?" he thought.

He heard her reply, "Yes, Zeke, it is possible. You are hearing me in your mind. That is how I am communicating with you."

Even though this was how he heard her, he wasn't afraid. He also wasn't fearful of the ghost-like way she floated. There was warmth and a feeling of love that surrounded her. It made him feel completely comfortable. He wondered if she would be able to answer the only question he had on his mind. "Why is Grandpa lying in this casket?" As this thought went through his mind he saw Moon Willow nod her head to indicate she understood his question.

He heard her voice again in his mind. "I have a message for you, Zeke. Your grandpa is going to get sick. He's going to have a heart attack."

"How do you know this?" asked Zeke, in alarm.

"I am one of your spirit guides, Zeke. I know everything about you and those you love. I know when new people will come into your life, and when people around you will depart the earth's plane and return home. I am one of many spirit guides who are always watching and guiding you.

We are here to illuminate the teaching. The teaching of which I speak is the 'Universal Power'. This is the power that connects one's mind and spirit to the universe's divine white light, the highest energy form in the entire universe. Some refer to this energy as 'God'; others refer to this energy by another name. In the end, they are all referring to the same thing.

I am the spirit guide that speaks directly to you. Sometimes I will speak through your dreams. But once you have accepted me and have grown in your beliefs, I may communicate with you in different ways. You may hear my voice, but you won't see me. Or I will show you letters, numbers or other symbols. There are yet other forms of communication that will be revealed to you when you are ready.

"How will I know it's you if I don't see you?" asked Zeke.

"Please understand, Zeke, it takes a lot of energy to make myself visible to you, which is why I will not always appear to you. For now, though, I visit in your dreams until I feel you are ready for more.

When you awake from this dream, you will not remember all the details that I am sharing with you. Throughout your lifetime, certain people will enter your life. These people will teach and guide you from the earth's plane. You will always have the choice whether or not to listen and learn. You have been given a gift, Zeke. It is up to you to accept it and use it.

As you continue on your journey, Zeke, you will encounter believers and non-believers. Some people will not accept the teaching, or will only grasp some of the teaching. Others will embrace it, and some people will go beyond to teach others. One of your hardest lessons will be not to judge any of them. Instead, accept everyone as they are and always show love and understanding.

Zeke listened very carefully to everything that Moon Willow said. It was a lot of information to take in at once. As he watched her, it appeared that she was starting to fade. "Wait," he thought, "I have one more question. When will my grandpa have the heart attack?"

Moon Willow smiled as she answered, "I may not answer that for you."

"But I thought you said you knew everything?"

"I do, Zeke. I know the answer, but I can not tell you."

"Why not?" pressed Zeke.

"You are on what is called a 'need-to-know basis.' I am not allowed to interfere with events, and may only share certain information with you. I have done all I can do here. I have shown you the same message twice about your grandpa. The rest is up to you. If you believe what I have showed you, you will share your dream with your grandfather.

"I was going to tell Grandpa today, but Griffen was there."

"There will always be obstacles in your life. That is why the choice will be up to you."

"I don't like this," cried Zeke. "It's too much responsibility!"

As Moon Willow began to fade away, she answered, "I understand."

"What happens if I tell Grandpa and he doesn't believe me?"

"You can not control what he believes. It will be as it is meant to be."

"So, Grandpa is going to die?" All Zeke could see now of Moon Willow was an outline of a body form, which was now moving away from the casket.

"I did not say that, Zeke."

Zeke felt desperate for further guidance, as he shouted, "What should I do?"

"Believe in yourself, Zeke, and do what you feel you should do," answered the fading voice. The ghostly figure of Moon Willow and the white mist had disappeared. In its place was a very small ball of light.

"I don't want Grandpa to die," cried Zeke.

He watched as the small ball of light moved very fast across the church and then came back and stopped directly in front of his eyes. Hearing Moon Willow's voice again, he realized that this small ball of light was her. He listened as she once again spoke in a soft voice, except this time it was harder to hear her when she said, "I can only guide you, Zeke. The rest is up to you." Zeke blinked his eyes and in that instant the small ball of light disappeared. He knew she was gone.

Zeke woke up to a dark room. Slowly, he reached under his pillow. He felt it. His willow stick was still there. Maybe it was the willow stick that was making him have these dreams. Then he remembered when he dreamt that dream under the tree by Wilder Creek, he didn't have the willow stick with him. He let go of the willow stick and stared into the darkness. As his eyes adjusted, he looked at the clock. It was 2:35 a.m.

Not caring how late it was, he got up to tell Grandpa about his dream. Getting out of bed, he quietly made his way to the door. Barley moved behind him and he whispered, "Stay, boy. Stay!"

When he reached his grandparents' bedroom door, it was closed. He knocked a couple of times and waited for the door to open or to hear a voice tell him it was okay to enter. Nothing happened. He slowly opened the door and whispered, "Grandpa, Grandma, I need to talk to you." A light went on by their bed and he saw Grandpa sit up.

"What's wrong, Zeke?" asked Grandpa.

"I really need to talk to you."

"Sure, son, come sit down." Zeke sat on the edge of Grandpa's bed and blurted out everything from his dream about the church, the coffin and the heart attack. When he finished, he waited for his grandpa's response.

At first, his grandpa just looked at him. Zeke noticed that he had a startled look on his face. He wondered if he had done the right thing by telling him.

Grandpa reached for Zeke's hand. "Son, it's going to be okay," he reassured him. "I'm fine. I'm feeling good. I haven't had any chest pains and I have a doctor's appointment coming up soon. While I'm there, I'll ask the doctor to check my heart."

Zeke sighed with relief. "Okay, Grandpa. I hope you're not angry with me because I told you about the dream."

"No, Zeke, I am not angry with you. I'm glad that you told me. If you have another dream, I want you to tell me. Okay?"

Zeke nodded in agreement.

"Now, you go back to bed and try to forget about the dream. Everything is going to be fine," encouraged Grandpa.

Zeke hugged him. He loved Grandpa so much, and just the thought of losing him made him feel sick inside. He suddenly felt like a big burden had been lifted from his shoulders.

"You know, Grandpa, one of the things I remember about the dream was that Moon Willow said I had been given a gift. I'm not sure what she meant, because it doesn't feel like a gift. Instead it feels like a curse or something. I hope that I don't have any more dreams like the one about you."

"I agree. It sounds like a lot of responsibility," responded Grandpa.

"I hope that you don't either," said Grandma.

For the first time, Zeke realized that Grandma was also sitting up and had been listening as he told Grandpa about the dream. He ran to the other side of the bed to hug her as well.

Feeling better, Zeke said good-night to his grandparents and quietly shut their bedroom door as he left the room. Returning to his bedroom as silently as possible, he found Barley right where he had left him. From the noise that Griffen was making, he knew that he was still in a deep sleep.

Zeke climbed back into bed and relaxed. Morning would arrive before he knew it.

Chapter 12

As soon as he heard the rooster, Zeke woke up. He was surprised that he was the first to awaken that morning, especially since he hadn't gotten a lot of sleep during the night. "Maybe I'm getting into a new routine…a farmer's routine," he thought. He raised his head from the pillow to see where Barley was. He didn't need to look far. Barley was lying at the end of the bed.

Knowing that it was his turn to take Barley out to do his morning business, he shifted his legs to get out of bed. That was all he had to do. Barley stood up, wagged his tail vigorously, jumped off the bed and headed straight for the bedroom door.

When Zeke arrived in the kitchen he noticed that the light was on. He could smell coffee, but no one was around. He went immediately to the back door to let Barley out. He waited for Barley and then the two of them returned to the bedroom. When he opened the door he saw that Griffen was awake.

"Morning," said Zeke, as Barley jumped on Griffen's bed to give him some morning licks.

"You're up bright and early," said Griffen.

"Yeah, as soon as I heard Bud, I was awake. His cock-a-doodle doodling is better than any alarm clock."

"Are Grandpa and Grandma up?" questioned Griffen.

"I think so. The kitchen light was on and I could smell coffee, but I didn't see anyone. Maybe Grandpa was out gathering eggs. I took Barley out and came back as soon as he was done."

Journey with Zeke

"Okay," said Griffen. "Maybe he's getting more stuff for the camping trip." Rising, Griffen did a few morning stretches. "Boy, I slept like a log. I was so tired."

"You can say that again," teased Zeke. "You snored all night."

Griffen laughed. "I always snore when I'm really tired. It must be the fresh country air. Anyway, I'm going to take a shower, get dressed, and eat some breakfast. I'm starving!"

Zeke had already changed his clothes while they were talking. "I'm going down, see you in a few."

"Yep," acknowledged Griffen while he yawned. "I'll be right down."

Barley followed Zeke back to the kitchen. This time he could smell bacon cooking as he descended the stairs. Boy, that smells good, he thought to himself as he entered the kitchen.

Grandma was sitting at the table and Grandpa was standing at the stove flipping some bacon. Both of them said good morning when they saw Zeke.

"Morning," replied Zeke. He wasn't sure how he was going to feel when he saw them this morning, with everything that had happened during the night. But he actually felt good. It was like a heavy burden had been lifted, and he felt cheerful.

After breakfast, they loaded all the camping and fishing gear onto the ATV. Nobody spoke about what had happened during the night. Zeke wondered if the whole thing had been a dream, including talking to his grandparents. Was he going crazy? However, at this moment he didn't really care. They were going camping.

Zeke started to get in the back seat. "Oh, no you don't," said Grandpa. "It's your turn to drive."

"Really?" replied Zeke, surprised. He glanced over at Griffen. He expected some sort of complaint.

"Yep, it's time for you to learn," chuckled Grandpa.

"Are you kidding?" teased Griffen. "He'll put us in a ditch in no time." Everyone laughed.

Zeke got into the driver's seat. Griffen plopped in the back with Barley, while Grandpa climbed into the passenger seat so he could teach Zeke how to drive. "When you want to go, push there," said Grandpa, as he pointed to the gas pedal. "When you want to stop, push there," as he pointed to the brake. "That's all there is to it, except for the steering. Just don't jerk the wheel, and try not to put us in any ditches. Got it?"

Zeke grinned from ear to ear. "Got it!"

"Then what are you waiting for? We've got some camping and fishing to do. Hit that gas pedal and let's go!" whooped Grandpa.

Zeke put his foot on the gas pedal and pushed down gently. With a jerk they were moving. Zeke screamed with excitement, "This is fun!"

With a few directions, Zeke progressed through the woods toward the planned campsite.

"Park Old Bessie right over there," pointed Grandpa. Zeke was a natural ATV driver. Other than hitting a couple of holes in the ground and bouncing everyone around, the ride had been pleasant.

The scent of the pine trees surrounded the camping area. Grandpa knew the woods well. He had been camping around here since he was a young boy. Not much had changed through the years, except for some trails being added by quad and motorcycle riders.

After Zeke parked, they set about getting Old Bessie unloaded. The boys chose the site where they would pitch their tents. In no time, tents were set, campfire wood was gathered, and the fire pit was secured. All they had to do now was enjoy the rest of the day.

"I'm ready to start exploring!" announced Zeke. The boys loved to explore their surroundings. They loved discovering a new bug, snake, butterfly, bird or tree. They even liked exploring rocks. Fishing would wait until tomorrow morning because it was too late in the day.

"I have a special place that I want to show you boys," said Grandpa. "Griffen, you're driving this time."

Everyone loaded back onto Old Bessie. Grandpa gave directions by pointing which way to go. Griffen drove slower than his normal clip. Twenty minutes later, a huge hill covered with trees came into view.

Journey with Zeke

"Wow!" exclaimed Griffen, over the noise of the motor. "Let's ride to the top!"

"Can't let you do that, son. That hill is actually an Indian burial ground. It's sacred and must be respected. It's been here for hundreds of years," explained Grandpa. "But we can walk it!"

Griffen parked Old Bessie on the east side of the hill. He was amazed at the hill's size. It was like a small mountain! He looked around to see if there was a path to the top, but he didn't see one. "Maybe there's a secret path to the top and only Grandpa knows the way." Curious, Zeke asked if the Indian burial ground was haunted. Grandpa smiled. "Some believe it is. I've heard a few stories in my day." Grandpa took the lead and started up the hill. When he had walked about half way up, he stopped to rest.

As the boys waited for Grandpa to recover, they started exploring their surroundings. Zeke turned over a large rock. When he was lucky, he sometimes found a salamander or some other creature underneath, escaping the heat of the day in the cool dark ground. When he stood up, it wasn't what he found under the rock, but rather what he felt that made him speak up. "I'm getting a strange feeling."

Griffen wasn't about to let this opportunity slip, "You are strange, that's why!"

Zeke ignored him and looked to Grandpa for feedback. He put the rock back where he found it and walked over. "Look at my arm! All the hair is standing up. Plus, I suddenly felt the temperature change."

"There we go. He's a rocket scientist. We walked out of the sun into the shade, and he noticed that the temperature changed," snickered Griffen.

Zeke threw Griffen a dirty look. It was his turn to become annoyed with his brother. Sometimes Griffen thought he was just so funny. Zeke was being serious and he was happy that Grandpa was with them to intervene.

Grandpa thought he understood what Zeke was feeling. He leaned in close to the boys as he dramatically whispered, "You are feeling the spirits of the hill."

Griffen studied Grandpa's face for a few seconds. He was trying to decide if he was playing a joke on them or if he was being serious. From what he could tell, he was being serious. "Spirits?" he asked.

"Some people say that when a spirit is near, the air around you gets colder and the hair on your body stands up," answered Grandpa.

"Serious?" asked Griffen. "Are you saying that there is a spirit around us?"

Grandpa nodded. "Yes, I am. However, the choice is yours to believe or not."

"I definitely believe," admitted Zeke. "I can actually feel it."

Griffen wasn't so sure. He moved closer to his brother. "Let me see your arm."

Zeke raised his arm so that his brother could see the hair standing up. Still not convinced that they weren't trying to play a joke on him, Griffen challenged the fact that the hair on his brother's arms was standing up. As far as he knew, Zeke could have rubbed his arm with something to make this happen, like when hair has static electricity and it stands on end. "Stop it. You're not scaring me," stated Griffen with a hesitant laugh. "Remember, I know how to tell the scariest ghost stories of all!"

"I'm telling you the truth," said Zeke. "I'm not making any of this up and I'm not trying to scare you. I'm telling you that I don't understand why I felt the air suddenly turn cold or why the hair on my arm is standing up."

Griffen was about to respond when he felt something icy cold all over his body. Jumping back, he screamed, "That's not funny!"

Grandpa and Zeke both looked at him. Neither one said a word, but they looked at him a bit strangely. Grandpa wanted his grandsons to accept what they were experiencing and not be frightened by it. He rolled up the sleeve and said, "Griffen, come look at my arm. The hairs are standing up. I feel the coldness, too."

Griffen's face went white. He froze at the thought that there really were spirits around them. He wanted to run. Just as he started to turn and head back down the hill, he heard a voice say, "Don't be afraid."

"Did you hear that?" asked Griffen.

"Hear what?" asked Grandpa.

"I just heard a voice say, 'Don't be afraid.' Griffen looked all around him and then franticly looked at Zeke for validation. "It's the same voice that I heard at home, and the same voice that I heard in the cemetery."

Zeke listened, but wasn't sure how to reply. Besides, he had just made his own discovery. "I just saw a small dark shadow move over there!" exclaimed Zeke, as he pointed past some trees. "It was close to the ground!"

"It sounds like something is moving over there," added Griffen.

Grandpa walked over to investigate. "Look, boys! I think I know what made the shadow and the noise," announced Grandpa. He pointed to the area the sound had come from. As all three watched, they could hear a rustling in the undergrowth as whatever it was started running toward them.

Griffen immediately turned and started running down the hill. He wasn't about to stick around while something was coming for them. He had taken about eight running steps, when he heard his brother giggle.

"Barley!" squealed Zeke.

Everyone had been so caught up in the temperature change and the hair standing up on their arms, they had completely forgotten about Barley. They gave him some hugs after he bounded toward them.

"Come on, boys. I've rested long enough," commented Grandpa. "We're almost to the cave. Turning to look at Griffen, he added, "That's if you're not too scared that a ghost is going to get you."

"Cave? What Cave? You didn't say anything about a cave," questioned Griffen. He had always wanted to explore a cave!

With the announcement that they were heading toward a cave, the boys instantly forgot about their recent experience. The coldness disappeared and none of them looked at their arms again. Their attention had been diverted, which was exactly what Grandpa had hoped would happen. He knew the boys would keep on asking questions, and he simply did not have all the answers. Never in a hundred years did he expect that they would experience what they just had. He had been to the Indian burial grounds many times, and not once had anything like that happened to him. He had heard stories, but he hadn't experienced it himself until today. Wait until he told his few close friends! They would probably think he was crazy and kid him, the same way they had teased others in the past. He wasn't about to admit this to his grandsons, but what happened had spooked him. It was an experience that he would rather not experience again.

When they had almost reached the top of the hill, the boys saw a small, dark opening. Anxious to explore what was inside the cave, Griffen ran to the opening and started to poke his head inside.

"Griffen, don't go inside," yelled Grandpa, who was still about thirty feet behind. "Why not? I want to explore," stammered Griffen. Barley started sniffing the ground near the entrance.

"It's not safe," answered Grandpa, as he hustled to his grandson. "That cave has been there since I was a child. I've heard that parts of it have collapsed. A few years ago a couple of local boys got trapped in there. They came to this area to camp. When they didn't return, a search party formed and the boys were found trapped inside. Thankfully they were okay. They had a few cuts and bruises, and I believe one of them had a broken leg, and the other boy had a broken arm."

"Can I just peak inside?" pushed Griffen. "It can't hurt just to look inside, can it? It's no fun to see an actual cave and not get to go inside."

"I would prefer that you didn't," answered Grandpa firmly. Obeying, Griffen moved away from the cave entrance and went over to sit on a rock with a sigh. Grandpa and Zeke joined him.

"Have you ever been inside, Grandpa?" asked Zeke.

"Yes, once, a really long time ago."

"What was it like?" inquired Zeke.

"It was dark and damp. And before you ask, no, I didn't find any bones. I have to admit, though, there was a funny smell. There was a group of us, including some expert cave explorers. They made sure we had the right safety equipment. Plus, we wore helmets with a light built into them so we could see well." He peered over at his grandsons to make the point that you should be prepared for cave exploration.

"The cave started out level and even and there was light coming in from the entrance, but soon we were descending down into darkness. We couldn't see very well and if it wasn't for the lights we had with us, we wouldn't have been able to see a thing. In some places, the rock was slippery with moisture and we had to be careful lest we slip and fall. The further we went the darker and more treacherous it became. We followed the cave for as far as we could go, which took us over an hour. The cave just came to an abrupt end. We turned around and made our way back. The experts had been in the lead the entire way. We all expected to find some bones, but we didn't. So I don't know if anyone was ever actually buried in the cave, or if they were buried at the top of the hill. We're heading there next. You'll be able to see some really old stones where someone chiseled dates into them."

"Let's go see them," suggested Griffen.

They made their way up the rest of the hill and Grandpa showed them the chiseled rocks that he had described. Besides the rocks, everything else looked exactly like you would find in the woods. Feeling the boys' boredom, Grandpa decided it was time to head back to the campsite.

They made their way back down the barely visible trail that they had made going up. When they reached the bottom they headed toward Old Bessie. Barley ran ahead and jumped aboard. Suddenly Griffen stopped, holding out his arms to block the others. Looking around, he asked, "Did you hear that?"

"Here we go again," laughed Zeke, as he played along. "Hear what?"

"I just heard someone yell the name 'George'," said Griffen.

Smiling, Zeke looked at his brother, "Wow, you keep saying that I'm weird, but look at you. Who's George?" asked Zeke

"Duh….that's Grandpa's name!" Griffen replied.

"Oh yeah," Zeke responded dejectedly. How could he have forgotten that?

Everyone looked around, but they didn't see anyone.

Griffen looked at his brother. "I'm not making this up. I'm telling you that I heard someone yell Grandpa's name."

"It's okay, Griffen, I'm sure you heard something or you would not have said so," said his grandfather reassuringly.

Zeke shook his head. He wondered if it was Moon Willow yelling his grandfather's name, and started to become alarmed. What would that mean? Is he about to have a heart attack? What would they do if his grandfather had a heart attack out here in the middle of nowhere?

They resumed walking, but had only taken a few steps when Griffen stopped again. "I just heard your name again, Grandpa! Stop. Listen."

Grandpa did as Griffen asked. He heard it, too! Then Zeke heard it! The sound was really faint, but he turned to where he thought the voice was coming from. As he did, he saw two riders on horseback galloping toward them. Recognizing his neighbor, Al, Grandpa raised his hand to acknowledge the riders.

Zeke was relieved that it wasn't Moon Willow yelling his grandfather's name, and that his grandpa probably wasn't about to have a heart attack, but wondered who the riders were.

"Who are they, Grandpa?" asked Zeke.

The riders continued to approach. Grandpa smiled and said, "Al is my neighbor. The young lady with him is his granddaughter, Catori. They call her Cat for short."

Once Al and Cat reached them, they dismounted. Grandpa and Al shook hands. "Nice day for a ride," said Grandpa. Al nodded in agreement. The boys stood behind Grandpa as they watched and listened. They seemed to know each other pretty well.

Al winked at his granddaughter as he continued the conversation with George. "Cat's staying with me this week. I've been teaching her about nature and how to connect with the land. We're going to camp tonight and are hoping to catch some fish tomorrow."

Griffen, who had already checked out the dark-haired, beautiful girl, stood quietly and listened to the conversation. She appeared to be about his age. Zeke, who was not shy like his brother, jumped at the chance to join in the conversation.

"Cool! That's what we're doing. We're camping tonight. You should camp with us. We brought our fishing gear, so you could go fishing with us tomorrow, too!"

While Al laughed at the young man's enthusiasm, Grandpa quickly introduced his grandsons and extended the same invitation as Zeke.

Al looked at his granddaughter. He knew that she might feel a little awkward camping with boys her age. She was 15 years old. As much as he knew about her, there were many things he did not know. He understood that teenagers at this age could be particularly sensitive. Not wanting to offend anyone, he stepped over to ask her privately, "How do you feel about camping with these folks tonight?"

Cat was a beautiful girl. Her long, dark hair and olive brown skin complimented her brown eyes. She carried herself with a quiet confidence and intelligence. However, she really wasn't that comfortable around boys. It seemed that whenever she was around a cute boy, she didn't know what to say. She glanced over at Griffen. She guessed that he had to be right around her age. And, yes, she thought he was very cute. After a moment's hesitation, she responded, "Sure, I think it will be fun."

"It's settled then," said Al. "We'll join you. Are you camping close to here?"

Grandpa noticed that Al had a concerned look on his face. "No, we're camping a couple miles away from here. I just brought the boys over to see the Indian burial grounds." Grandpa saw Al's face relax and understood why he had been concerned. In order to respect the land and the spirits, camping around the burial grounds was not an option.

"Wow, I'm impressed," said Al, looking at Grandpa. "You walked a couple of miles?"

"No, we brought Old Bessie. We were just heading back to get her."

Al laughed. "Of course, how is she doing?"

"Great! The boys love her. In fact, they took her out yesterday and were gone most of the day."

"She's just down yonder, around the bend," chirped Zeke. "Come on, we'll show you."

Al and Cat mounted their horses and followed the group. Grandpa walked alongside Al. It had been a while since they had seen each other. This was a great time to catch up. The boys led the way. Cat thought about catching up and joining the boys, but then decided against it. Griffen thought about going back and joining Cat, but wasn't sure what he would talk about with her, so he stayed with Zeke.

They rounded the bend and there sat Old Bessie, right where they had left her. They chuckled when they saw Barley in the driver's seat.

"Hey, Al, will your horses get spooked if I start her up?" said Grandpa.

"Oh, no, feel free. They're used to tractors and all kinds of noises."

"Okay, then, just follow us."

Grandpa started up Old Bessie with a roar, and the horses trotted behind. Fifteen minutes later they were back at the campsite.

Al noticed that the fire pit had been secured and the firewood gathered. He motioned for Cat to join him directly across from the tents that were already set up.

Griffen noticed that Cat was taking a large bundle from her horse. "Bet that's her tent," he thought to himself. He walked over and offered to help.

Cat was caught off guard. She certainly hadn't expected this cute boy to offer his help. "Sure," she said as her face turned pink. For the next ten minutes, Cat and Griffen laughed and picked on each other until the tent was secure. Little did they know that this was the beginning of a special friendship that would last for years.

With the tent secure, Cat turned to find her granddad. There was still plenty of daylight and she wanted to go for a walk. She saw him standing with George and Zeke by the campfire. Motioning for Griffen to follow her, they walked over to the campfire to join the group.

The mood was light as everyone got to know each other. Still wanting to go on a walk, she asked if anyone else wanted to go with her. She hoped that Griffen would. She liked him and wanted to spend more time getting to know him. It actually surprised her how relaxed she felt around him.

"I do!" yelled Zeke.

"Oh, great," thought Griffen. He really didn't want his brother tagging along on the walk. Cat looked over at Griffen, waiting for him to respond. He smiled. She knew at that point, without him saying a word that his answer was yes.

"Great idea and enjoy your walk. We'll cook dinner," said Grandpa, winking at Al. "Dinner will be ready at 6:00 p.m. After we're done eating, you can do the cleanup while we relax."

Griffen turned to look at Cat. Just looking at her gave him a feeling he had never felt before. He didn't know how to explain it. He was used to cleaning up after dinner and he wondered if she was, too. That did not concern him. Right now all he wanted to do was spend more time talking with Cat.

"Come on, you guys!" called out Zeke. "Let's go this way!" Cat and Griffen followed him into the woods.

Chapter 13

During the first couple of minutes the older two walked in awkward silence while Zeke rambled. He kept pointing out various aspects of the woods, animals, and other things he saw. Finally, he noticed that his brother and Cat were not saying anything so he asked, "So, Cat, what school do you go to?"

"I go to South Central High." I'm a sophomore this year."

"Where is South Central High? I haven't heard of it before."

Griffen smiled as he listened to his brother question Cat. Even though he really didn't want his brother to tag along, now he was happy that he did. If there was one thing his brother was good at, it was getting a conversation going and keeping it going. Now all he had to do was listen and learn. This way Cat wouldn't think he was being too nosy. He was already excited to learn that Cat was a sophomore, just like him.

"It's in town. I live a couple of miles from Granddad. I visit as often as I can, especially since my grandmother died last year."

"I'm sorry to hear that," replied Zeke. Griffen also offered his condolences.

Cat politely smiled. "Thank you, it's been hard. I loved her very much and I really miss her!"

"We can relate," said Griffen.

"Your grandmother passed too?"

"No," answered Griffen, "but she has cancer. Mom is with her in Florida right now. She beat it once, but it came back."

Journey with Zeke

Cat's face suddenly looked sad. The boys had no way of knowing that her grandma had fought a long battle with breast cancer. She had gone to the doctor for a routine check-up when the doctors found a mass. After all the testing was completed, they had diagnosed her with stage four cancer. The boys' situation sounded too familiar. It brought back a lot of memories.

Griffin went on to explain, "Grandma B was diagnosed with breast cancer two years ago. When she was finished with all of her treatments and was strong enough we celebrated by going to Universal Studios to see the new Harry Potter Theme Park."

"Really?" exclaimed Cat. "I love Harry Potter. I read all the books and I saw all the movies. I especially liked the way the last movie ended. So was the park anything like the movies?"

"It was! It was amazing! They had the coolest ride, too, where it was like flying in a Quidditch match. I could have stayed there all day," bragged Griffen.

"I bet! I want to go someday. I think it'd be so much fun," giggled Cat. She paused for a moment then added. "I'm sorry, we were talking about your grandma and I changed the subject. Please tell me more.

Griffen was taken aback by her kindness. He knew a lot of girls, but the ones he knew were usually more concerned about themselves than anyone else. This was refreshing. He knew there was something special about her. Maybe that was why he felt an immediate connection to her.

Griffen turned toward Cat as they continued to walk. "No need to apologize. I changed the subject, too. Anyway, last weekend Zeke and I went camping with Dad. On the way back home, he told us Grandma B's cancer was back."

"I am so sorry to hear about your grandma. I will keep all of you in my prayers. I'm a strong believer in prayer and miracles."

Both boys thanked Cat for her offer to pray. They, too, understood the power of prayer. It had worked the last time for Grandma B. Every morning and night, both of them, as well as other family members and friends, prayed for their grandma and she had recovered.

"Hey, Cat, I don't want to change the subject again," said Zeke, "but I have a question. Your granddad said he was teaching you how to connect with the land. What did he mean?"

Cat's face lit up. She always felt a special connection with nature and she loved sharing it. Granddad had taught her a lot. Knowing it would take her awhile to describe, she looked around and saw some rocks nearby. Pointing to the rocks, she suggested they sit down.

Zeke immediately took off running and reached the rocks first. This gave him the first choice of where to sit. Looking over his shoulder he saw Cat and Griffen were getting closer to him. He had to make a quick decision. Jumping over a few smaller rocks, he chose the biggest rock, placing him directly in the sun. He wanted to be sure that Griffen wasn't able to sit on the biggest rock, plus it seemed the most comfortable. Quickly sitting down, Zeke waited for them to join him.

Griffen chose the shaded rock directly across from Zeke, while Cat sat down on the empty shaded rock between them. She noticed that Zeke was squirming around and understood why.

"Zeke, would you mind sitting over here next to your brother? That way, I can talk with both of you without having to turn my head back and forth."

Without hesitation, Zeke agreed. Beads of sweat were already forming on his forehead. He jumped down from the rock and sat next to Griffen.

Cat wanted to make sure she explained everything the way her granddad had taught her. She didn't like to answer a question by asking another question first, but she felt she had no choice. She didn't want to insult them, but she needed to know where to begin.

Smiling, she looked at Zeke first. "I'm going to answer your question, but before I do, I need to ask you both a question, okay?"

"Okay," responded Zeke, then Griffen.

"Do you believe that everything is energy?"

Griffen and Zeke looked at each other. Griffen didn't want to admit that he had no clue what she was talking about. After all, he had just met

Journey with Zeke

her. He didn't want to make a fool of himself, so he remained quiet and raised one eyebrow to show his interest.

Zeke pondered the question. He had taken science in school and they had talked about energy. However, just like Griffen, he wasn't sure what Cat was asking. He wanted to be sure. "Well, like, what do you mean?"

Cat thought for a moment and then responded, "Zeke, you were just sitting on a rock that had been exposed to direct sunlight. What did it feel like when you touched it?"

"It was warm," he replied, as he wiggled his bottom around indicating that actually it was hot to sit on.

"Griffen, your rock was shaded by a pine tree. What did it feel like when you sat down?"

"It was cool."

She smiled as she continued. "Both of you just experienced energy. The rock itself is energy. It's a part of the earth. Mother Earth, as some refer to her, is full of all different types of energy. Some of the energy is natural and some of it's manmade. My granddad has taught me that energy is what makes things happen. Just like now, the sun is giving off light and heat energy. That's why the rock you sat on, Zeke, was warm to the touch. It was being heated by the sun and had absorbed the energy.

"Griffen your rock is also energy, but because a tall pine tree is standing in the sun's energy path, the tree is receiving the heat energy it needs to grow, instead of the rock. In return, the tree's energy is producing oxygen which is what we need to breathe. The tree is also producing shade for your rock, which is keeping it cooler than the rock in the sun."

"Okay, I get it," said Griffen. "I remember learning in school that we eat food because our food contains energy. Our body requires energy and we use the food's energy to work and play. And I understand the part about manmade energy. Gasoline is manmade energy that we use to fuel the cars we drive."

Cat smiled and nodded her head in agreement. The trio continued to talk about different types of energy and compared what they knew.

"Okay," said Zeke, "everything is energy...but I still don't get what your granddad meant."

Cat giggled, and Griffen loved her giggle. He hadn't known her long, but he sure did like her.

Cat chose her words carefully. "First, please know that Granddad understands so much more than I do. He visits the woods a lot. He says it helps him connect with the universe. He visits even more since Grandmother died. Sometimes we sit in the woods and listen to the wind whistle through the trees. Other times we sit by the river to listen to the water. He's told me this practice helps to restore positive energy to our soul."

"Wow, that's neat," responded Zeke. "You mean if I'm feeling sad or angry, I can sit by the water or someplace quiet and I'll feel better?"

Griffen could tell this could be a very long conversation.

"Don't answer that," he interrupted. "It's 5:30 p.m. and we need to start back to make sure we're back by 6:00 p.m." Everyone agreed.

As they walked, Cat let Zeke know that the answer to his question was yes, but it required more than just sitting by water or someplace quiet. It required that the mind connect with the universe. The questions continued back and forth as they made their way back to camp. The three were becoming friends fast.

"Hey, do you smell that?" asked Zeke. "I think I smell hamburgers. Hey, fire is energy, too!" And with that comment, he took off running toward the campfire.

This was the first time that Griffen and Cat had been left alone. They watched in the distance as Zeke ran up to the campfire. Beginning to feel a little uncomfortable by the sudden silence between them, Cat commented, "Your brother sure can run fast."

Feeling relieved to have something to talk about, Griffen quickly answered, "He sure can. He competes in track meets at our school. Last year he set a new school record."

"That's great! You must be so proud of him."

"I am," responded Griffen.

As they walked the last several feet in silence, Griffen reflected to himself, "Before today, I don't think I ever admitted that I was proud of my little brother. I guess I really am proud of him, even though he can be so annoying."

Chapter 14

THE EVENING AIR BEGAN TO cool as the sun approached the horizon. With their bellies full from a great dinner, everyone relaxed in their chairs around the campfire. Zeke noticed that Al kept glancing at the sun as it set in the west, so he did the same thing. Every time he noticed that Al was looking, he would also. Not finding it very much fun, he decided to put his brother on the spot. "Griffen, I think you should tell one of your world famous ghost stories."

Griffen shot his brother a look. He knew full well that Dad had asked him not to tell any ghost stories because of Zeke's dreams. Just because Dad wasn't here, didn't mean it was okay to do it. He could feel everyone's eyes looking at him. He was not going to go against what his dad had asked of him.

Grandpa sensed that Griffen was uncomfortable with Zeke's request. Maybe he was embarrassed to tell the stories because of Al and Cat. He decided to offer some encouragement. "My grandson is really good at telling ghost stories. I've heard some really scary ones over the years. I'm ready for a good ghost story. How about you, Al? Cat?"

"I don't know," said Al, skeptically. "It's got to be really, really scary! Are you up to it, Griffen?"

Griffen looked at Cat and noticed her smile. Looking back at the camp fire, he answered quietly, "I really do like telling ghost stories, especially really, really scary ones, but Dad has asked me not to for a while." Glancing quickly over at his brother, he continued, "Zeke's been having these weird dreams and Dad doesn't want me to scare him with my stories."

Journey with Zeke

Zeke was instantly upset. Why would Griffen share that? That was private information and he didn't appreciate Griffen sharing anything about his dreams with strangers. Now they would think he was weird. Embarrassed, Zeke barked, "I have not! Tell your old ghost stories, I don't care!"

Al could feel the friction between the brothers. Trying to ease the tension and hoping to put Zeke at ease, he said, "Hang on, Zeke. Perhaps instead of telling ghost stories, we should talk about your dreams and what they mean. I have dreams all the time. All of us do. It's natural. There are many messages and lessons in our dreams. We just need to understand what they're trying to tell us."

Zeke sat back down and stared into the fire. He wasn't sure how to respond. He wanted more than anything to understand his dreams, but he didn't want anyone to laugh at him. His brother did that enough. Remaining silent, he continued staring into the fire.

"I'll go first," offered Al, "if that's okay with you, Zeke."

Zeke nodded his head, as he muttered, "Go ahead."

Al began, "Like I said, I dream all the time. Last night I dreamt that a white owl came to my room, landed on my chest, and then disappeared right before my eyes. Shortly afterward a white wolf appeared, looked at me, and did the same thing the owl did. It disappeared. When I woke up this morning I quickly wrote down what I saw in my dream. I didn't want to forget what I had dreamt, which many of us do."

Hearing the mention of a white owl and a white wolf peaked Zeke's interest. He studied Al and asked, "Wow! Were you scared?"

"No, I wasn't scared. Catori and I come from a long line of Hopi Indian ancestors. My great, great-grandfather was a Hopi Indian medicine man. He was well respected in his tribe. A medicine man had many responsibilities; one of them was to know what different animals represent and what our dreams are trying to tell us. I was taught that when an owl appears in your dream, it means wisdom. When a wolf appears in your dream, it means guidance. Color is also important. Both the owl and wolf where white in color, which represents cleansing."

Zeke listened intently, just like everyone else. He was extremely interested in what he had just heard, but he was also baffled. As far as he could tell, there was nothing scary or unusual about Al's dream. It sounded a little hokey to him. Picking up a long stick he started poking and stirring the ashes of the fire. He could hear Al talking, but he wasn't paying close attention anymore.

Al could tell that Zeke's interest was gradually waning. He knew the next statement would pull him back. "Zeke, actually, my dream was about you."

Startled by what Al had just said, Zeke stopped stirring the ashes and looked up. "Your dream was about me?"

Everyone laughed, while Al answered, "Yes, it was."

"How could that be? You just met me today."

Al smiled. "That's one of the beauties of understanding a dream. When you don't understand a dream, it's a mystery. But with knowledge and experience you'll learn how to unlock the mysteries of your dreams and understand what they mean.

Truly intrigued, Zeke encouraged Al to continue.

"I told you the meaning of the owl and the wolf and explained that they represent wisdom and guidance. I also said that they were both white, which means cleansing. I've learned that when I have this type of dream, I will meet a person soon that needs my help. Zeke, you're in a place in your life where you're beginning to experience vivid dreams. Is that correct?"

"Yes."

"You need help with understanding your dreams, is that correct?"

"Yes!"

"That's the reason you and I met today. We crossed paths because we were supposed to. I'm to help *cleanse* you of your fears about having dreams that you don't understand. I will help *guide* you with the *wisdom* I have about dreams."

At first no one said anything. Even though Cat's granddad had taught her many things about energy and the land, she had never heard him speak like he did tonight. She was amazed by his knowledge.

Griffen was letting everything he heard sink in. If everything Al said was true, then he should have never made fun of Zeke and his dreams. Now that he had a better understanding, he could relate better to what his brother was going through. He wondered if Al would also be able to explain to him why he was hearing voices and what that really meant.

Right behind this thought, Griffen heard a voice in his head say. "Now is not the time. Your time will come soon." Startled by the voice, Griffen looked around to see who was talking. No one was looking at him. In fact, no one was saying anything. He decided to remain quiet about it and see what would happen next.

Zeke could feel tears forming. Finally, he felt that he had connected to someone who truly understood him and what he had been going through. After all, this was not something he had asked for; it had just started happening. Yes, it was scary. Yes, he did fear his dreams. And yes, he was ready to talk about it!

"In my dreams there's an Indian lady. She says her name is Moon Willow. Do you know who she is?" This time his brother didn't make any smart remarks. Instead, he sat quietly waiting for the answer.

Al nodded his head. "I know Moon Willow. She is a spirit guide. She's very wise. She'll help you on your life's journey, Zeke. You'll find as you age that you have been given a special gift. It may not seem that way now, but I promise you, in time you will understand that your gift can help unlock mysteries of the universe and help you better understand and connect with the spiritual world."

"I don't know," said Zeke shaking his head back and forth. "It doesn't feel like a gift. Instead it feels like a curse. Some of my dreams are scary and I don't like it!"

"Why don't you start by telling me about one of your scary dreams? Perhaps I can explain to you what your dream is really about."

Zeke looked over at his grandpa. He didn't want to just blurt out that the last few dreams were about him, unless he said it was okay. "You tell him, Grandpa."

All eyes were on Grandpa. Looking back at Zeke, he felt a sense of pride about his grandson. He appreciated that Zeke was being careful about his feelings. "Thank you, Zeke, but since you had the dreams, I think you should be the one to talk about them. Don't hold back any of the details or emotions. Tell what you saw and how it made you feel."

Zeke took a deep breath and then began relaying to everyone the dreams about his grandpa. He told them about seeing him lying in a casket, and that he tried really hard to get to the casket, but he could never reach it. He also told them how Moon Willow was in his dreams and how she said that he needed to warn his grandpa.

When Zeke had finished, Al looked at George and said, "I'm concerned about Zeke's dream. Have you been feeling okay?"

Grandpa responded to Al's question, "Yes, I've been feeling fine. Zeke did tell me about his dreams. I'd already scheduled a doctor's appointment next month for my physical. I promised Zeke that I would have the doctor check my heart, too.

Al completely understood how delicate the situation was. He had been in situations like this many times before. Often he had to make the choice of whether or not he believed enough in his dream to actually talk to the person his dream had been about. He accepted that some people would view him as either crazy or weird. Yet, he clearly understood that others would trust what he shared with them. What worried Al more was how he would feel if he didn't say something, if his dream came true. It was a lot of responsibility and he took it seriously. He had learned through experience to keep an open mind.

When he felt that his worrisome feeling grew strong enough, he would usually find a way to share his dream. This often required careful thought. Sometimes he prayed for further guidance. Other times, based on his feelings and timing, he would make contact with the person to ask them how they had been feeling. He was very careful not to alarm the person or scare them. Instead he would make general conversation and find a way to bring up the right questions to help deliver the message in his dream. The most important lesson he had learned was *what was meant to be, would be, no matter what.* This was one of those times. He would need to approach this situation with ease and not alarm George or Zeke.

"George, since Zeke has had this dream twice, I'd suggest that you call your doctor on Monday and see if you can move your appointment to an earlier date."

Griffen, Zeke, and Cat sat frozen in their chairs. Never in a hundred years did Griffen think that they would be having this type of conversation around a campfire. There was a part of him that was scared and just wanted to change the subject. This was actually scarier than any ghost story he could have told. He found it interesting how everything was working out. First Dad tells him he can't tell any ghost stories, and now they were discussing something he thought was much scarier than anything he could have made up. This was too weird.

Grandpa sat forward in his chair. He looked at Al first and then at Zeke. He didn't like being the center of attention, but he trusted his friend. "OK, I promise. I will call the doctor on Monday and see if I can get an earlier appointment."

Zeke felt relief wash over him, "Seriously, Grandpa, you're going to call?"

"Yes, Zeke, I promise."

"Thank you," said Al. He too felt better. He had accomplished what he needed to without revealing all the details. What he didn't tell them was that when he had his dream the night before, in addition to seeing the white owl and white wolf he had seen a young boy standing over an older man. The man was lying on the ground holding his chest like he was in pain. He hadn't seen their faces, just dark silhouettes. Upon waking, he had done what he always did. He grabbed the paper tablet and pencil that he kept on the night stand, and wrote down these words:

Wisdom; Guidance; Cleansing; Young boy; Man; Heart Attack

Al understood very well that nothing happened by coincidence. Everything happened for a reason. You didn't always understand what it meant when it happened, but if you paid attention, the answer was always revealed. He also understood that many of his dreams were protection dreams. They were not meant to scare him. They were to prepare him for what was going to happen.

He never knew when the answer would be revealed; sometimes it was a short period of time. Other times, it was revealed after a long period of time had passed. He knew that if he kept having the same dream, it was even more important for him to pay attention. In that situation, most likely the event would happen in a shorter period of time. Sometimes more detail would be given when the dream was repeated. This was another reason that he wrote down all his dreams. He was able to go back and look at his notes. He would gently remind George in the morning of his promise to them. He was sure that he would not forget, but it was better to be safe than sorry. Someday he would explain all of this to Zeke.

Zeke rose from his chair and walked over to his grandpa and gave him a big hug. "I love you," said Zeke. "I was so worried about you."

"I know you were," said Grandpa, returning the hug. "I love you, too! Now don't you worry anymore, okay?"

"I won't," answered Zeke.

Cat watched as Grandpa and Zeke gave each other a hug. She was happy for the two of them. She was also feeling really tired and wondered what time it was. As she felt a yawn coming on, she knew it must be about 10:00 p.m., her usual bedtime. She didn't want to miss any of the conversation, but she knew her granddad well. He had always taught her that people can only absorb so much information at any one time. She thought they had reached that point. It had been very interesting. Yawning again, she stood and walked over to her granddad. "Going to bed," she announced as she reached to give him a hug. "Love you!"

Griffen was still trying to absorb everything he had just heard. Some of it made sense, but a lot of it did not. He wanted to believe, but it was hard. How was he supposed to get his head around the fact that someone could have a dream and then it was their responsibility to figure out what that dream meant? Heck, he didn't even remember his dreams half the time! He wondered why some people remembered their dreams more and why some people didn't. At this point, he didn't want to think about all that. He too was tired. After giving his grandpa a hug, he headed for the tent. Zeke followed.

Al and Grandpa remained at the campfire with Barley. Grandpa was in deep thought. He knew it was common knowledge that Al had special talents. Some townsfolk said he was a psychic, and others referred to him as a medium. He had also heard Al called some names that were not so nice.

From time to time, Grandpa heard stories about how Al's dreams had come true. He knew that some of the town folk would seek Al out and ask for his advice, or sometimes they would request a reading. He had heard other stories, mostly from his wife, of how Al would connect someone from the afterlife with a loved one still here on earth. The only strange thing that Grandpa could relate to was the time when he had been in the horse barn and for a split second he had seen an Indian lady standing in the corner of the barn. Now he wondered if that had been this Moon Willow spirit they were talking about.

One thing he knew for sure, though. Al had been his friend for over 30 years. They shared common interests in politics, hunting, farming, and sports. Their wives had been friends, too, until Al's wife, Evelyn, had passed. Not once had Al ever talked to him about anything like what he heard tonight.

Grandpa looked away from the fire and toward Al. Having been in such deep thought, he didn't realize that Al had been speaking to him. He refocused, and listened as Al repeated himself. "You have a talented grandson. He has been given a gift. If he chooses to develop and nurture the gift, he will be able to help many people in his lifetime. I would be more than willing to work with him and help him, as best as I can, but only if you and Zeke's parents agree."

Grandpa could not speak for his son or his son's wife. He honestly didn't know what they would say. As far as he knew, they were only aware that Zeke had dreams that scared him.

"Thank you, Al. I appreciate your offer. It means a lot to me and I know it would mean a lot to Zeke. It sounds like there's a lot of responsibility to all of this. When my son comes to pick the boys up, I let him know of your offer and let you know what he says."

"Fair enough," responded Al.

Chapter 15

Zeke was careful when he crawled into the tent. Griffen had entered first and since it was a small tent, there really wasn't much room. Actually there was just enough room for the two of them. Originally he thought that he would sleep under the stars by the campfire, but the night air had turned cool and he knew it would be better to sleep inside. Besides, in here the mosquitoes wouldn't eat him up so badly.

Once he was settled into his sleeping bag, he started thinking about everything that Al had said. As his mind raced, he came to the conclusion that the universe was full of mystery. He wondered if there was even one person who truly understood all the mysteries that the world and the universal held. "Impossible," he thought.

He could hear conversation still taking placing outside at the campfire. He wondered if Al and Grandpa were still discussing dreams and what they meant. He strained his ears to listen, but couldn't make out exactly what they were saying. It was muffled from this distance.

His mind drifted back to everything discussed around the campfire. He wondered if he should tell Mom and Dad about his dreams and what Al had said. It really didn't matter right now, because his parents weren't there. All that mattered now was that he was feeling tired. He wondered how someone turned off their mind when there was so much to think about. However, it wasn't something he had to really worry about, because soon, even with his mind whirling, he fell asleep.

Zeke felt his body floating again, except this time he was not at the church. Instead he was on a side of a mountain with a breathtaking view of a magnificent waterfall. Even though he had only heard the voice a couple of times, he recognized it immediately. He smiled and continued to listen.

"Zeke, I want to share another message with you," said Moon Willow.

"It's important that when you wake up, you don't think of this message as a bad dream. It will appear that way, if you don't understand the true meaning. Instead, I want you to concentrate on what you are seeing. When you wake up you will have a decision to make; a decision that only you can make."

The scenery suddenly changed. He was walking down a path with his brother, Al, Cat and Grandpa. They were walking single file toward a lake. Each of them carried a fishing pole. Grandpa also carried a bucket. Grandpa showed them a perfect spot to fish off the bank of the shore. He turned around and saw Al talking on his cell phone. He heard a noise and when he turned around he saw Grandpa lying on the ground, holding his chest. Then all of a sudden he was walking down the path again, headed to the lake. The dream repeated itself. The second time he saw more detail and paid closer attention to everything he saw. The dream ended again with his grandpa lying on the ground with his hands over his chest.

As the dream continued to replay again, he felt no emotion toward what he was seeing. He felt disconnected from the events happening around him. He thought that was strange, but didn't question it. His dreamed changed again and he was back at the mountain. Once again, he heard Moon Willow's voice. "Zeke, when you awaken, you should only talk about this dream with Al."

Zeke felt something touch his leg. Waking up suddenly, he saw that Griffen was unzipping the tent door. "Hey, where are you going?" he asked.

"Sorry, I didn't mean to wake you," responded Griffen. "I smell bacon!"

Zeke sniffed the air. Yes, it was definitely bacon. "Cool. I'm starving."

Zeke quickly unzipped his sleeping bag, which was easy to do since his brother wasn't lying next to him. Following his brother out of the tent, he was met by the morning's early sunrise. He stretched and looked toward the campfire. He saw Cat and Grandpa cooking.

"Wow, that smells good!" exclaimed Griffen as he approached. "What can I do to help?"

Cat looked up from turning the bacon. Seeing the boys, she teased, "They're alive!" Giggling, she added, "You two are in charge of the toast."

"Funny," responded Griffen as he smiled at her. Even in the morning she was strikingly beautiful. He felt something stir in his stomach.

"Funny?" thought Cat. She wasn't sure of his comment. Was he referring to her "They're alive" comment, or was it because he didn't want to make the toast? Boys could be so hard to understand. She reached behind her for a loaf of bread and threw it at him.

Wanting to tease her back, Griffin called out, "Hey, what an arm! Trying out for quarterback?"

Cat thought, "Yep, we're going to get along just fine," as she let out a little giggle.

"One or two slices?" he asked.

Zeke was happy that Griffen was busy flirting with Cat and not paying attention to him. He wanted to talk to Al about the dream he had last night. He was sure Al would be able to help him understand it. He had some thoughts of his own, but wanted to be sure. "Where's Al?" he asked.

"He's in the woods", answered Grandpa. Pointing to the trail that Al took. "Would you please go tell him it's almost chow time?"

"What's he doing in the woods?" quizzed Zeke.

"He's meditating. Or should I say he's 'replenishing his positive energy."

Cat chimed in. "I've already finished my meditation. It's so refreshing. You should try it, Zeke. Go find Granddad. I'm sure he would love to show you how it works."

Zeke didn't have a clue what Cat was talking about. Meditation? Not wanting to get into a full-blown conversation about whatever meditation was and wanting to talk to Al anyway, he simply replied, "Okay," as he took off running in the direction that Grandpa had pointed. Once in the woods, he looked to the left, and then to the right, but he didn't see Al anywhere. He continued running down the trail.

Suddenly there was a burst of brilliant red among the trees that caught his attention. He stopped. A red cardinal flitted from one tree branch to another. He noticed how graceful it was. As it took flight, Zeke's eyes followed the bird. It landed again a few yards away.

It was then that he noticed Al sitting on a rock in a clearing in the middle of a group of trees. "Wow!" he thought, "if I hadn't stopped to watch that cardinal, I would have run right past him!"

He noticed how well Al and his clothing blended into the woods. Zeke wondered if he did that on purpose or if it was just coincidence. Approaching slowly, he noticed that Al had his eyes closed. His feet were flat on the ground and his elbows were bent with his palms facing up. "Is that what you do when you meditate?" thought Zeke. If it was, it looked pretty easy. He observed quietly, waiting for Al to acknowledge him. Al never moved or opened his eyes.

Not wanting to interrupt, Zeke turned to walk away. As he turned, Al said, "Good morning, Zeke."

Startled, he blurted out, "Cat and Grandpa wanted me to let you know that breakfast is almost ready. Sorry to bother you."

"Oh, yes, I've been smelling bacon for a while now. Figured it was just about ready. Come join me for a minute." Al gestured with his hand for Zeke to sit beside him on the rock. Zeke walked over and sat down. As soon as he was seated, Al asked. "Have you ever meditated?"

"No," answered Zeke quietly.

"Then today will be a new experience for you. Do you remember last night when I told you that you had a special gift?

Zeke looked directly into Al's eyes before he nodded.

"What I'm going to teach you today is how to stay connected with your inner self."

"My what?" questioned Zeke, as a puzzled look came over his face.

"Your inner self," repeated Al. "Let me start by explaining what you and I are. When people look at each other, or we look at ourselves in the mirror, what we are looking at is our physical body. Do you agree?"

What a silly question, thought Zeke, before he answered, "Yes."

"I think we would also agree that bodies come in different sizes and shapes. Some bodies have light-colored hair and others have dark-colored hair. Some bodies are covered with a light-colored skin and some have olive or darker skin. I am sure you have noticed that some bodies are skinny while some are heavier, some short, and some are tall. Different people have different types of bodies and body parts. You have brown eyes. Your friends may have blues eyes or green eyes.

"Zeke, would you agree that our bodies are what people see every day and we are recognized by our features?"

Zeke nodded his head to agree.

"Would you also agree that inside your body you have organs, such as your heart, brain, liver and kidneys, as well as blood, muscle and bones?"

Again, Zeke shook his head yes.

Al continued with his teaching. "What I have just described to you are all things about the body that can be seen. However, there is something else inside our bodies that can't be seen. It is beautiful and intelligent. It's called our soul. Our soul is many things, but the most important thing to remember today, is that our soul is energy."

Zeke followed everything that Al had just said until he reached the part about the soul being energy. He wondered if he should stop him or just let him go on talking. He made the decision to stop him.

"Soul? Energy? I'm kind of following you, but not entirely. Yesterday on our walk, Cat talked a little bit about energy. She said something about rocks having energy, as well as the sun and the trees. Is it like that?"

"Cat is a smart girl and she has learned a lot," beamed Al. "What she was telling you is that everything on earth and in the universe is some form of energy. Yes, a rock is a form of energy, as are the sun and the trees. Water is energy, and the moon, and the stars, the land, clouds, birds, animals, plants; whatever you can think of is a form of energy.

"Zeke, your body is also a form of energy, and the soul that is located inside your body is energy."

"So everything I see and touch is energy. Is that right?"

"That's right, Zeke."

"Cool! But I'm still confused about one thing. All the things that you named are things that I can see. If the soul is also energy, why can't I see it?"

"I'm impressed, Zeke. Excellent question! Let me start by saying that for as many people who believe they have a soul, there are just as many who don't. Those who do believe, in many instances, feel that way because of their religion. Others have learned through an experience that has changed their life, like a near death experience. Still others have learned from someone who has a strong belief system in a higher being. Sometimes it's a combination of these factors."

Al paused for a moment before continuing. "Today, I am doing two things; sharing with you my beliefs, and teaching you that there is more to the body than what the eye can see. It all depends on your beliefs, and the faith you have, whether or not you'll believe in what I'm sharing."

Zeke pondered what Al was saying. Wanting to make sure that he understood, he said, "I've heard about the Holy Spirit in church. Is that the same thing?"

Al smiled. "Yes, it is. Do you believe in the Holy Spirit?"

"Sure, I do. So does Griffen, Mom, Dad, and lots of people."

"Then we believe in the same thing. Now let's take it a step further. Have you ever seen the Holy Spirit?"

"No, can't say that I have."

Journey with Zeke

"Neither have I, yet I know in my heart that the Holy Spirit is real. I believe this because I have faith and trust in what I believe. I have a faith and trust that without actually seeing it, an energy greater than me exists in the universe."

"Wow!" exclaimed Zeke. "I get it! But…what does this have to do with meditation?"

Zeke watched as Al looked up to the sky and then slowly looked all around him before he looked backed at Zeke. "Meditation provides a way for our body's soul to send and receive energy vibrations with the universe, to and from a higher energy form than what we are. When we relax our body and our mind, it allows our soul to release negative energy so it can be replaced with a positive energy. You can meditate anywhere. I really enjoy meditating in a forest, or next to a body of water. In the forest, it's really quiet and I'm able to sit among natural energy. Natural energy is a conduit for positive energy, just like water. When I feel the vibrations from the land, the trees, from water, or all three, it helps calm my mind, and it connects me to the land. It leaves me very relaxed and completely refreshed. You want to try?"

"I do, but what about breakfast? And, I really need to tell you about the dream I had last night."

"I understand," said Al. "I'll show you the specifics on how to meditate later. Let's head back for some breakfast. On the way you can tell me all about your dream."

Zeke quickly relayed all the details of his dream. He told Al how it had changed from Grandpa being in a casket to all of them fishing and Grandpa lying on the ground with his hands by his chest. He also told him about seeing Al on a phone, but didn't know exactly what was being said. "The part that really bothers me is Moon Willow told me that I would have a choice to make and I needed to concentrate on what I was seeing in my dream. What in the world does that mean? I don't get it! I already told Grandpa about my other dream and that he should go to the doctor and so did you. He promised he would go soon."

Al put his hand on Zeke's shoulder. "It's going to be okay, Zeke," he reassured.

"No! No! No!" screamed Zeke. "I am so frustrated." Feeling completely overwhelmed he let it all out. "I have a brother who makes fun of me. One minute he tells me he understands and then the next he's telling me not to tell anyone. I have a dad who isn't listening to me, and a mom who would listen, but she needs to be with Grandma B because of her cancer. I know I scared Grandma Cook when I told her about the dreams. I could tell by the look on her face. Now Grandpa may be having a heart attack. Then there's this Spirit Guide ghost, or whatever she is, who keeps coming to me in dreams. I hate it! I just want it to go back to the way it was before I started having all these dreams – before we visited the cemetery and I brought home that stupid willow stick. I'm going to throw that thing away. I was going to before, and I didn't. This time I'm really going to do it!"

Al looked at Zeke with sympathetic wisdom. "I understand the frustration you're feeling, Zeke, I really do. It's a lot of responsibility. However, I promise that as you begin to understand how all the pieces fit together, you will feel much better. With knowledge, acceptance, and patience, you will be rewarded. You really have been given a gift. I know it doesn't feel that way now, but one day it will."

Zeke looked up at the sky. He could feel the tears coming again. "I never cry, and yet that's all I seem to be doing these days. I'm tired of it!" he thought. Hearing a noise, he looked down the trail and saw Cat and Griffen running towards them.

"You okay?" asked his brother when he got closer.

"Yes," answered Zeke, "I'm fine."

Cat was concerned, looking first at her granddad and then at Zeke. "We heard you screaming. It sounded like, "No! No! No!"

Zeke stood firm, and in a snippy tone he blurted out, "I don't want talk about it. All I want to do is eat some breakfast. I'm starving." To make his point, he started running back to camp.

Griffen didn't like his brother's attitude. What right did he have to be snippy with him? All he did was ask if he was okay. As he turned to run after his brother, he felt someone grab his arm. "Let him go," said Al.

Al brought Cat and Griffin up to date on what had happened and why. Griffen once again paid close attention, especially when his name was mentioned and how his brother felt. By the time Al was done explaining everything, he had forgotten that he was upset with his brother. Instead he felt sad about the way he had made his brother feel. He loved Zeke, but knew that he didn't always show it. From this point on, he would be sure not to make fun of him, at least about his dreams.

Giving Zeke some alone time, the trio slowly walked back to camp. When they arrived, he seemed to be in a better mood. He was eating and joking with Grandpa. Nothing more was said about the events of the morning.

Al grabbed a plate, sat next to Zeke, and ate breakfast. Griffen, Cat, and Grandpa started the cleanup, as soon as they had finished. Zeke and Al whispered back and forth for a couple of minutes and then joined in the cleanup. With the last dish cleaned and put away, Grandpa, who had been whistling, announced, "Let's go fishing!"

The lake wasn't that far away so they made a decision to walk. As they turned the bend and could see the lake, a funny feeling came over Zeke. He tried to ignore the feeling, but it wouldn't go away. Why did everything look so familiar? He had never been to this lake before, and yet he seemed to recognize the place.

"If you want the best fishing spot on the whole lake, we need to head this way," said Grandpa as he turned to the left. Trees lined the lake and it was beautiful. The open land gave way to a single path between the lake and the trees. Grandpa led the way, followed by Griffen, then Cat, with Zeke and Al bringing up the rear.

When they reached Grandpa's favorite fishing spot, everyone set about getting the fishing poles ready. They placed the bait on a shaded rock because they knew how important it was to keep the bait out of the sun. There was a little bit of a drop-off from where they were standing to the water below. It was a perfect spot for casting.

Zeke suddenly realized why everything looked so familiar. This spot was exactly what he had seen in his dream last night. He felt fear washing over him. "No!" he thought, "It can't be!" He looked all around, trying to find something that didn't look the same as his dream, but he couldn't.

"Should I say something?" he thought with panic. But before he could speak, he heard a cell phone ringing to his left. It was Al's. Just like in the dream! Al was on the phone. That's when he heard a commotion to his right and he saw Grandpa lying on the ground with his hands up by his chest. He watched as Griffen and Cat ran toward him. He stood perfectly frozen. His body would not move. He wanted to run to Grandpa also, but his feet wouldn't move.

He heard a loud scream, and then an echo of screams. He didn't even realize that the scream had come from him. Time seemed to stop. All he could think about was his dream and how what he had seen in his dream was now coming true. He felt his body shaking and it took him a few seconds to realize that Al was the one gently shaking him.

"Everything's okay, Zeke," said Al in a reassuring voice.

Al's gentle shaking had forced Zeke's eyes to focus, and he pulled away from Al and looked for Grandpa. He was surprised and relieved to see him sitting on a rock staring at him. Without hesitation Zeke ran to him, throwing his arms around his grandpa to give him a big hug. Grandpa felt the force of Zeke's hug and had to brace himself so he didn't lose his balance.

Concerned about his grandson's reaction to his fall and not understanding why he had reacted the way he did, Grandpa asked, "You okay, Zeke?"

"Am I okay? Are you okay?"

"I'm okay," replied his grandfather with a little chuckle. "At my age I have to be a little more careful. When the grass is wet, it's slippery. Silly old me, I slipped and fell, but I'm okay. No broken bones." Again, chuckling, he added, "May have a few bruises later though." Everyone except Zeke laughed.

Grandpa looked his grandson in the eyes. "Zeke, I didn't mean to scare you."

"I know, Grandpa. I just thought that you had a…" He stopped talking. Did he actually want to say what he was thinking?

Grandpa knew what he was thinking. "I know, son, you were thinking I was having a heart attack, like in your dreams, right?"

"Yes! I had another dream last night. It was different than the dreams before, but what just happened is what I saw in the dream. I saw Al on the phone and you lying on the ground with your hands by your chest. So when all that happened, I guess I freaked. I don't want anything to happen to you!"

"I know it's scary, Zeke," replied his grandpa. "However, now that you know I'm okay, let's put it behind us. We've got some fishing to do!"

They spent the next couple of hours fishing. Zeke was happy to be the first one to snag a fish. He quickly forgot about his dream and enjoyed the rest of the morning. By time they were done, they had caught twenty fish. They gathered their gear and headed back to the camp site.

After lunch, Cat, Zeke, and Griffen spent the rest of the afternoon exploring the trails. They returned, as Grandpa had asked, by 3:30 p.m. Grandpa wanted to be home in time for dinner. They quickly repacked the tents and cleaned the campsite. The only way someone would have known that they had camped there was if they noticed the remains of the fire pit.

Griffen helped Cat secure her tent to her horse. He hated to see her go.

"I had a great time, Griffen. It was wonderful to meet you."

Griffen smiled. "I had a great time, too. You've got my number. Call me or text me any time you like."

Cat reached out and gave him a hug. "I certainly will," she said.

Griffen felt exhilarated. He wondered if she would actually contact him after they were home. He watched as Cat and her granddad trotted away on their horses. He wanted her to turn around one more time to give him some small signal that she liked him, as much as he liked her. Just when he thought that she wasn't going to, he saw her turn. With a smile on her face, she waved. Griffen's face lit up and smiling from ear-to-ear, he waved back.

"Come on, Griffen!" yelled Grandpa. "You're driving us back if that smile of yours doesn't get in the way." Griffen couldn't wipe the smile from his face. He had been happy many times before, but somehow this was different. Just as he reached Old Bessie, he heard his phone. "Could it be her already?" he thought. He quickly grabbed his phone and immediately recognized the number. "Hi, Dad."

"Well, you certainly sound happy," said his dad. "You must be having a good time."

"Oh yeah, Dad! It's been great," responded Griffen. "Zeke and Grandpa are here with me. We went fishing and exploring today and we're getting ready to head back to the farm. Hang on. I'm putting you on speaker."

Everyone said their hellos. Dad explained that he would be arriving the next day around 2:00 p.m. They would leave on Saturday morning to head home. He updated them on Mom and Grandma B. Everyone was happy to hear that Grandma B was doing well and Mom would be home the following Wednesday.

The boys told Dad about meeting Al and Cat, exploring the Indian burial grounds, camping, and catching so many fish.

"You clean 'em, and I'll cook 'em tomorrow night," offered their dad. Then, speaking to Grandpa, he said, "Dad, if it's not too much to ask, would you invite Al and Cat for dinner? I'd really like to meet them."

Grandpa said he would.

"Great! I'm looking forward to seeing you all. Love you, and I'll see you tomorrow!" Everyone returned their love.

Griffen put the phone back in his pocket and fired up Old Bessie. Thirty minutes later, they were back at the farm.

Chapter 16

"**L**et's unload at the back door," suggested Grandpa, as he signaled for Griffen to drive around back. Griffen rolled to a stop at the back door. As he turned off Old Bessie, Barley raced toward the house. Grandma opened the door and like a flash Barley jumped up to lick her face. With his tail wagging wildly, there was no doubt that Barley was really happy to see her.

Grandma came out and helped them carry everything into the house. "I've got dinner ready. Let's eat first, and then you can take care of everything else."

During dinner, the boys talked about the camping trip, and explained how much fun it had been. When they reached the part about meeting up with Al and Cat, Griffen felt his excitement grow. He listened as Grandpa told Grandma about Dad's call and that he would be spending the night at the farm before heading home. Grandpa went on to tell her that Dad had asked him to invite Al and Cat over for a fish fry. "I'll give Al a call here in just a little bit to invite them," confirmed Grandpa.

Nobody mentioned Zeke's dream about Grandpa, or that Grandpa had fallen at the lake that morning. Grandpa had asked them not to say anything. He wanted to tell her when he felt the time was right. He knew that she would fret and want him to go to the doctor. He felt fine – no need for her to worry.

After dinner, Zeke went outside to play with Barley. Grandpa went to the man cave in the barn, and Grandma sat down to watch TV and do a little knitting. This left Griffen alone on the front porch to think. He wanted to text Cat to ask if they were coming for the fish fry.

Lynette Teachout

"Should he or shouldn't he? What if Al had already talked to Grandpa? What if he hadn't?" He was driving himself crazy trying to decide what to do. That's when he thought, "I don't have anything to lose. I'm doing it!"

Griffen opened his phone and typed, "Fish 2mrrow. 6. Can u come?" He hit send, and listened as his phone confirmed the text had been sent.

He had no more than closed his phone, when he recognized the sound of a return text. Anxiously opening his phone, he saw Cat's name and the return message, "Yes!" He felt a flutter in his stomach and his heart racing. "Come on, tomorrow!" he thought.

Zeke was getting tired. It had been a long day. Dreams, camping, fishing, chores, and now playing with Barley had worn him out. He was ready to relax. As he came through the front door with Barley, he saw his grandma sitting in her chair with her eyes closed. On her lap rested her knitting needles. Not wanting to wake her, he led Barley upstairs to the bedroom as quietly as he could. Barley went over to lie down on his blanket. Zeke grabbed his laptop. He had not opened it since he had been there. He wondered if there was a wireless internet connection. "Only one way to find out," he thought. He typed in the address to Facebook. Most of his friends were on there. He liked reading the posts, and Facebook's message system was a great way to keep in touch. Within seconds he saw the page launch. He entered his login name and password. He was in. Looking on his wall, he started reading the posts.

Jimmy Tower: *2marow?*

Andy Culver: *3*

Jimmy Tower: *k*

He had told his friends that he was going camping and fishing. Now would be a good time to catch up. Short and to the point, he posted: *Fishing & Camping Great! Barley!*

Within seconds the return posts were made.

Caleb Brown: *Cool. When u coming home?*

Zeke Cook: *Saturday*

Caleb Brown: *time*

Zeke Cook: *dk*

Caleb Brown: *call me game*

Zeke Cook: *k*

Jason Snyder: *Barley*

Zeke Cook: *new puppy*

Caleb Brown: *Yours*

Zeke Cook: *No*

Jason Snyder: *send pic*

Zeke Cook: *k*

Zeke grabbed his phone and took a picture of Barley sleeping on his blanket and posted the picture. He had just logged off when he heard the front door slam.

"Bet that woke Grandma up," he thought. "Come on, boy," he said, as he called Barley to follow him. When he reached the living room, he saw that Grandma had indeed awoken and was talking with Griffen. Barley laid by Grandma, while Zeke went to the opposite end of the couch where Griffen was seated. The three of them chatted until Grandpa came in the house at 9:00 p.m.

"Working late?" quizzed Grandma.

"Not exactly, I talked on the phone with Al for a while, and then watched some television. I fell asleep during Wheel of Fortune and just woke up." He gave her a sheepish grin.

Grandma laughed. "I thought maybe that was the case. I was going to give you until 9:30 and then I was going to send the boys after you."

Grandpa blew her a kiss and changed the subject to Al and Cat. "Good news, Al and Cat are coming for dinner tomorrow night. That should make you really happy, Griffen."

Griffen could feel his face turning warm. He hoped that nobody else noticed his face turn red. That would be even more embarrassing. He nonchalantly replied, "Glad they're coming." Turning his head toward the TV, he pretended that he was watching the program. Actually, he didn't want to discuss what he was feeling with anyone, at least not yet.

"And Zeke," continued Grandpa, "Al said his offer stills stands. He is going to talk with your dad tomorrow night about mentoring you to help you understand your dreams."

Grandpa filled Grandma in about Zeke's dream and that he fell earlier that day. When he had finished, Grandma walked over to him and gave him a hug. "Are you feeling okay now?"

"I'm fine. I don't want you to worry or fret about it! I'm going to bed." He gave Grandma a quick kiss on the cheek, and left the room.

"You know, Grandma, I don't know what it is, but since I've been here I keep going to bed early. Maybe it's the country air? I'm so tired right now that I don't think I can walk up the stairs." Zeke laughed at what he had just said.

Grandma laughed with him. "You go get yourself a good night's sleep."

Zeke went over and gave Grandma a hug and said good night to Griffen. Once he reached the bedroom, he quickly undressed and threw himself down on the bed. He hardly remembered his head hitting the pillow.

When Griffen entered the room a couple hours later, he noticed Zeke tossing and turning. He wondered if he was having another one of his dreams. Gently, he shook him until he woke. Whispering, he asked, "You okay?"

"Yeah, I'm okay, just tired. Something wrong?" mumbled Zeke.

"No," answered Griffen. "Go back to sleep."

Zeke felt like someone was watching him. He had told Griffen that he was tired, so why would he still be standing by his bed? Slowly, he once again opened his eyes and rolled over to face Griffen – except the dark form near him wasn't Griffen. He lay perfectly still and moved his eyes to see if Griffen was in his bed; he was. Now he knew for sure that this form wasn't Griffen trying to play a joke on him. He could feel Barley with his feet at the end of his bed. When he blinked the dark figure was gone. He sat up to be sure.

Lying back down, he looked at the clock. It was 3:00 a.m. He rolled back over to face the wall again. He felt the same feeling again. This time when he rolled back over he noticed the dark shadow standing at the end of his bed. He blinked a couple of times, just to make sure he wasn't imagining it. It was still there, except now it was starting to move closer to him.

Zeke wanted to scream, but for some reason was unable to. It was like he was so scared no scream would come. Whatever the dark shadow was, he didn't want any part of it. Yet, he was too scared to get out of bed. Watching the dark shadow he noticed that it started to change. He also heard a familiar voice say, "Don't be afraid." Zeke continued to watch the dark shadow turn into Moon Willow.

"Wow, you can do that too?" mumbled a bewildered Zeke.

"Yes," answered Moon Willow. "Spirits can appear in many forms, as you are experiencing. I am trying to teach you not to be afraid of the different forms when you see or feel them."

"Are you the one that Griffen has been hearing also? He told me that he has heard a voice tell him not to be afraid."

"Yes, it was me. However Griffen doesn't believe yet, nor is he accepting. Therefore, I will not be attempting to visit or contact him the same way I do with you. I will continue to guide him, but I will guide him differently than I guide you."

"Is it because he wouldn't put the willow stick under his pillow?"

"No, Zeke. You have already acknowledged that the willow stick had nothing to do with you being able to see or hear me."

"So, if I were to throw my willow stick away. Would that make you go away?"

"No, Zeke. I would still be with you. I know this may be hard for you to understand. As you grow you will understand more. Al has been sent to help you. You should accept his help."

"Really?" questioned Zeke.

"Yes, he is an old spirit and is very wise. As he told you, he comes from a long line of Hopi Indian ancestry. He has visited the earth's plane many times and is well connected to the energy of mother earth, animals, and the universe. He is a great teacher who is filled with love for others. Ask him all the questions you like. Listen to him. As you grow, you, too, will become very wise.

"I don't really know him. He told me that when Dad got here tomorrow he was going to talk to him."

"Yes, I know," replied Moon Willow. Then she added, "Your father will resist at first."

"What should I do?" questioned Zeke.

"Your father will change his mind in time. There is nothing more that you can do."

"How will I know?"

"You will know. Everything happens for a reason. When it happens, you will understand." Moon Willow started to fade away. Behind her was a brilliant white light, it was like she was fading into the light. He watched as she changed back into the dark shadow and then disappeared. As the tunnel of white light began to close he heard her say, "I will be with you tomorrow. It's important that you remember."

"Why?" thought Zeke. Very faintly he heard her say, "Grandpa."

Chapter 17

Zeke woke up with a start. He looked around the room. Griffen wasn't in his bed and neither was Barley. He heard faint laughter coming from the kitchen. Jumping out of bed, he quickly changed out of his pajamas and into his clothes. Grabbing his shoes, he threw open the bedroom door and ran toward the kitchen.

He was surprised when he entered the kitchen to see Griffen and Grandpa were already setting the table. He wondered why he hadn't heard Bud do his early morning routine of cock-a-doodle-doo. Walking up to the table he grabbed a chair, pulled it out and sat down. For a moment he wondered if he was still dreaming. It seemed he was moving in slow motion this morning. He could hear voices, but wasn't really paying attention to what was being said. He was concentrating on Grandpa. What did Moon Willow mean by "I will be with you tomorrow" and "Grandpa"?

Hearing his grandma's voice, he looked in her direction. He noticed she was flipping pancakes, and suddenly he could smell them. Blueberry pancakes – his favorite. He felt someone touch him on the shoulder, and turned to see Grandpa standing next to him.

"You still asleep, Zeke?"

"No, why?"

"Your grandma asked you to grab the milk from the refrigerator."

"Oh, I didn't hear her. I'm sorry." Zeke headed for the refrigerator to grab the milk.

Griffen in particular noticed that his brother was being exceptionally quiet. He could tell that something was really bothering Zeke, so decided not to razz him about it. He would talk with him later when they were alone.

As soon as breakfast was over, Grandpa and the boys headed for the barn. The hot August sun greeted them as soon as they walked out the door. It was going to be a scorcher. Nonetheless, they had to get the chores done. Both boys were excited about seeing Dad again, and chatted about it on their way to the barn.

The morning flew by. Everyone agreed that the chores would be done faster if they split up and each did their own. Griffen had gone to attend to the horse stalls, while Zeke had been assigned to taking care of the chickens. Grandpa was handling the cows.

August meant hot and sticky days on the farm. Today would be no exception, as the morning temperature was already in the low 80's. The only thing that made the day seem hotter was working inside a barn with no breeze to circulate the air. Griffen had tied a red handkerchief around his head to help keep the sweat from getting into his eyes. He had also removed his shirt. It helped a little, but not much. Whistling as he worked, he did not hear Cat enter the barn.

Cat had taken special care with her hair and make-up that morning. Normally on a hot day like this she would have thrown her hair into a pony tail and called it good, but today was different. She was seeing Griffen again and wanted to look her best. With the heat making her curls droopy and the sweat beading on her face, she wondered if she had made a mistake. Cat really wasn't a make-up person. She much preferred the natural look and had the type of natural beauty that made make-up unnecessary. As she stepped into the barn, she looked for Griffen. Hearing someone whistling, she followed the sound to the other end of the barn. Making her way past several barn stalls, she quietly walked up to the last stall to watch him while he cleaned the stall.

Cat enjoyed watching him work and noticed how his muscles moved. She let out a soft whistle and loved the expression on his face when he turned around and saw her standing there.

Griffen was totally surprised to see Cat. He knew they were coming for the fish fry, but wasn't expecting her until much later in the day. He quickly grabbed his shirt and put it on.

"You didn't need to do that," said Cat, smiling. "I was enjoying the view."

Griffen blushed and hoped that she would just chalk it up to the heat. "Wow, you're here early. Did you come to help me with the chores?"

"If I had known that you were going to need my help, I would have worn different clothes," Cat teased back. "Actually Granddad wanted to come early today to spend some time with your brother before you guys leave to go back home tomorrow.

Griffen nodded and kept smiling as he listened. When she finished he said, "Zeke's in the other side of the barn with the chickens."

Cat started laughing. "With the chickens… got it! I'll just go and let Granddad know where he can find him." She raised her hand and gave him a little wave as she turned and walked away.

Griffen didn't want her to go. He was almost finished with his chores. She had reached the barn door when he hollered. "Come back after you've found your granddad. I'm almost done here. We'll take a walk or something."

Cat turned around and gleefully hollered, "I'll be right back!" As she left the barn she saw Granddad walking toward her. She waited for him. Together they walked back into the barn.

Zeke had just finished his chores. He was having a rough morning. No matter how hard he tried to forget about his dream, he couldn't. He was eager to talk with Al and couldn't wait to see him later in the day. To keep his mind occupied until then, he decided to go see if Griffen needed any help. Entering that part of the barn, his face immediately lit up when he saw that Al and Cat were already there. As he got closer he could hear Griffen talking. Someone must have asked where Grandpa was, because he heard Griffen say, "Last time I saw him he was heading for the man cave. He said something about being hot, so he was going in to cool down a bit."

Al laughed. "Yeah, I don't know too many farmers that have an air-conditioned room in the barn. That's one of the smartest things your grandpa has ever done."

Lynette Teachout

"Hey, long time, no see," said Zeke, as he joined the group.

Al smiled at Zeke. He was just as happy to see him again as Zeke was to see him. When Grandpa had called the evening before to invite them to the fish fry, he had clued him in that Zeke's dad was not all that receptive to the offer he made to guide Zeke. Al wanted to make sure that Zeke knew that he was there for him anytime he needed him.

"I was just asking Griffen where your grandpa was. I heard he was hiding out in the man cave. Let's go join him! I'm sure it's a lot cooler in there than it is out here." Everyone agreed.

As soon as they entered the man cave they felt a rush of cool air. It was over 85 degrees outside and the cool air was a welcome relief. Grandpa was sitting in his lounge chair. He glanced over at the door when he heard it open. "Come in and join me," he said, with a grin on his face.

Al couldn't pass up the opportunity to poke fun. "Cat and I thought we would come early and help you with the chores. By the looks of you, I would have to say you're all done for the day."

Grandpa nodded in agreement. "It sure is a hot one out there. I may be old, but I'm not an old fool. You know what they say. If you can't stand the heat get out of it." The two men bantered back and forth for a few minutes while everyone listened. They would have continued, but the sound of the bell interrupted them. Even though Cat and Al were guests, they knew it was lunch time.

Grandma had not cooked a big lunch. She knew their appetites would be dampened by the heat. Besides, they would have plenty to eat at the fish fry later. When the group entered the house she greeted them with homemade lemonade and sun tea.

After lunch, Al asked Zeke if he would mind taking him for a spin on Old Bessie. Al knew that Zeke's dad would be arriving anytime and he still wanted to talk with Zeke alone. Zeke looked to his grandpa to make sure it was okay.

"You know where she is," said his grandfather, as he handed Zeke the key.

Zeke was excited. He didn't care how hot it was outside. Being able to drive Old Bessie again was an opportunity he wasn't about to pass up. The breeze would feel good, too.

"I'll be right back," he exclaimed, as the backdoor slammed behind him.

Grandpa noticed the puzzled look on Griffen's face, and quickly added. "Griffen, if you don't mind I would like to ask for Cat's and your help on a special project I've been working on in the man cave."

Griffen, who would have normally been upset at the thought of his brother taking Old Bessie without him and would have protested, instead replied, "Sure!" He had thought earlier about taking Cat to Wilder Creek for an afternoon swim. He had planned on asking Grandpa if he could take Old Bessie. No need to now. At this point all he really cared about was that Cat was there and he was able to spend more time with her.

When Zeke returned with Old Bessie, Al sat down in the passenger seat. "Where to?" asked Zeke.

"The lake," replied Al.

Zeke had driven back from the lake before and knew he could find his way there easily. With a touch of the gas and slight turn of the wheel, they were on their way.

Once they reached the lake, Zeke parked Old Bessie in the shade. "Let's go over there and sit," said Al, as he pointed to a row of shade trees close to the water's edge. They walked side-by-side, looking for a good place to sit down.

"Zeke, I've been thinking a lot about you being upset yesterday morning."

Zeke put his head down. "I'm sorry. I shouldn't have lost my temper like that."

"Hey, look at me, Zeke. You don't have anything to feel bad about. It's okay. I know it can be scary. I still clearly remember what I felt when I was about your age. I was confused and I certainly didn't understand my dreams. In fact, I remember feeling like you, that I had been cursed or something. I had asked, 'Why me?' I thought that I was the only one who had ever experienced dreams like you're having. Lucky for me, my grandfather had similar experiences and could talk about them with me.

"I remember one day in particular. I had spent the night at my grandparents' house. I'd had what I thought was a bad dream. I saw a red car go over an embankment. It hit a bunch of trees and then came to rest at the bottom of a ravine by some water. I could see the driver's face. He was older than me, but still young. That young man looked at me and said, 'My name is David and I need your help.' I woke up from my dream and didn't know what to think or what I should do. I didn't know where the accident actually happened. All I knew was that the car was red, it was at the bottom of a ravine and that the driver's name was David. Not a whole lot of information to go on.

"I decided to share my dream with my grandfather. He listened and said, 'I think I know the place you're describing. There is a stretch of road not far from here. If someone went off the road there, it would be very hard to find them. It's one of the only places where there is a ravine like what you're describing and it's not a well-traveled road. If someone really did go off the road in this area, they could be there for a really long time.'

"We left immediately to go check it out. First we drove by the area and did not see anything. We turned around and this time parked and got out of the car. Grandfather took the left side of the road and he told me to take the right side. We kept looking down the slope until the slope was gone and the land was level again. Turning around we walked back over the same stretch. I was just as focused as my grandfather. The trees were pretty thick making it hard to see if a car was down there somewhere.

"We were almost back to where we started, when I heard a voice say to me, 'Stop!' I looked over at grandfather and realized that he was not the one who had said it. The slope was really steep in this area. I stopped and looked around very carefully. Still not seeing anything, I started walking again. That's when I heard the voice again say, 'Stop!' Looking down where I stood, I noticed tire tracks in the gravel. I called for grandfather to come and take a look. He was taller than I and was able to see further down the slope into the ravine. He moved closer to the edge and then started down the steep incline. He hadn't gone far when he yelled for me to call 911. He had spotted the top of a red car.

"I dialed 911. Grandfather said the slope was too steep for him to go any further. He yelled, 'Hello! Is anyone there?' You could hear the echo of his voice return but no reply came. I said, 'His name is David. Call for David." He did. The third time grandfather called out David's name, we heard a faint reply. "I'm here. I'm down here."

"Grandfather yelled that help was on the way. When the rescue people arrived, they hooked up their safety ropes and went down the slope. It took them better than ten minutes to reach the car. None of us on the road could see what was happening because of the denseness of the trees. Over the walkie-talkie we heard the rescuer say, "There's a young man in the car. His name is David. Send down a gurney." When they brought David up, he looked really bad. He was barely conscious. They immediately put him in the ambulance and left with the sirens blaring.

Grandfather and I talked to a police officer who wanted to know how we found the car. At first I didn't want to say because I didn't think he would believe me, but my grandfather insisted that I tell him the truth. So I did. When I finished, the police officer who had been taking notes, paused, looked at me and said, "You know, son, you just saved David's life."

I have to admit that hearing him say that took me by surprise. I had been so focused on my fear that I had not realized the good that could come from my dream.

Anyway, the next day my grandfather and I went to the hospital to see how David was doing. We met his entire family. They said I was a hero because I had saved his life."

"Wow!" said Zeke, "That's pretty cool."

"It really is, Zeke, but the first step is to learn not to be afraid of your dreams. Instead you need to embrace them. Yesterday when you came to tell me breakfast was almost ready, you found me meditating. I meditate to allow the universal energy to work through me. It's a positive energy that is guided by the white light of the highest power the universe has to offer. When you are truly connected and you let the white light guide you, you will help many people."

"Can I tell you something?" asked Zeke.

"Sure, you can tell me anything."

"Last night I had a dream. In my dream Moon Willow was there and she told me that you were being sent to help me understand. Is that true?"

"It certainly is, Zeke."

"I don't understand how you will be able to help me. You live here and I live far away. How will you be able to help me with us living so far away from each other?" quizzed Zeke.

Al smiled. "Actually, it's pretty easy. Do you have a computer?"

"Yes, I do."

"Do you have Skype on your computer?"

"Yes, I do."

"There you go. We can talk anytime you want. You can either text me, instant message me, send me an email or contact me by Skype. Cat is a whiz with all this computer stuff. She has helped me to understand how it all works."

Zeke felt a sense of relief. He was glad that he had someone to help him understand his dreams. Feeling confident that he could share anything with Al, he decided to ask him one more question. "Moon Willow said the strangest thing to me before she left last night. She told me that you would be with me today. When I asked her why, she said it was because of my grandpa. Do you know what that means?"

Al slowly shook his head no. "One thing that you will come to understand is that we don't always understand the dream until after whatever was supposed to happen has happened. It's like connecting a puzzle. You can see all the pieces, but you don't see the picture until you have completed the puzzle. Does that make sense?"

"Yes, I just wished that I knew what it meant now. You know that I've been having dreams about Grandpa having a heart attack. I know that he's going to his doctor soon, but I'm still worried."

"I understand. However, you've done all that you can do. You delivered the message. It's up to the person to whom you delivered the message to act on the information, or not. You can't control that part. We live in what's known as the plane of choice. That means we have free will to make our own choices, our own decisions. It is now up to your grandpa to make his own choice and decide how he will handle what you have told him." It's also important that we not judge those who may not accept the message that we have delivered to them.

"What happens if he doesn't listen to me and something bad happens?" asked Zeke.

"It is just as important that we don't carry the guilt. This might be hard for you to comprehend right now, but I'm going to tell you something that you can think about. When you say 'something bad', you are probably thinking of death, right? You are worried that your grandfather might die. I believe that when someone dies, it only means that they are shedding their body form. We need the body form to sustain life here on the earth plane. When it is time for us to return home to heaven our soul is released from the body. Our soul goes home in spirit form. You will hear some people refer to heaven as the "afterlife". What they are saying is that they know our spirit form, our soul, never dies.

"Zeke, it's important to know that it is natural for us to think of dying as something bad. It is very natural to fear death. We are supposed to. I'll explain more about that to you later. All you need to understand right now is that when we lose someone we love, we miss them terribly. Our heart cries as we mourn not being able to see them, hear them, and touch them. Those who have a higher level of understanding acknowledge that in order for the soul, our spirit, to evolve, living and dying is a necessary process we go through so that our spirit will continue to grow. Even with this understanding, it is still very emotional and sad to those who have lost a loved one.

Al paused and took a deep breath. He wanted to be certain that he wasn't scaring Zeke. Death is always a sensitive subject. He didn't want Zeke to feel burdened or believe that he had been cursed.

"Zeke, things will be what they are meant to be."

Zeke's response was one of awe and surprise, "That's what Moon Willow said!"

"She's right," answered Al. "She's right."

"When your father gets here today, I'm going to ask for his permission to be a mentor to you."

Suddenly remembering what Moon Willow had told him, Zeke blurted, "Oh yeah, that was something else that Moon Willow mentioned. She said that he would resist at first."

Again Al smiled. "They usually do, Zeke. However, we must not be upset with him. Just as you have struggled to understand, he will too. It takes time. Sometimes an event has to take place before someone will change their mind. We must allow this process to happen."

"Okay," responded Zeke. "Because everything happens when it is supposed to, right?"

"That's right."

"Now I have something that I want to share with you," said Al. "I had a dream about you last night, and I would like to tell you about it."

"Me? Really, what was it about?"

"Do you remember when I told you that you had a gift that would help many?"

"I do." replied Zeke.

"That was what my dream was about. In my dream, I saw you helping others develop a better understanding of the universe and how the white light of the universe is always there to help them – how positive energy truly does have an impact on their lives."

"Okay, so how do I do this?" questioned Zeke.

"First, you need to start writing down your dreams and the messages in them. Then you need to share this information."

"Do I just write them on a piece of paper?"

"Yes", answered Al. "Keep a dream journal next to your bed. When you awake in the morning write down anything that you remember from your dream. Date the entry. That way you will be able to refer back at anytime and compare notes."

Journey with Zeke

Zeke thought this would be easy enough. But what was he supposed to write, when he didn't always understand the meanings of the dreams himself? He asked the question aloud, "How will I know what to write?"

"I will help you, Zeke. You will learn how to listen to your intuition and your heart. Both will help guide you. I will help and Moon Willow will help. Just remember to ask for the white light to guide you. What I mean by this is that if you have a negative thought, you will have to learn to change it into a positive thought. You will also have to learn to trust in yourself and realize that what may appear to be negative doesn't always mean it is something negative – like the dream you had about your grandpa lying by the water with his hands over his chest. It seemed like a negative dream, when in reality it was not. One more thing, Zeke - always thank your spirit guide."

Zeke nodded his head in agreement. He sat in silence for a moment taking in everything that Al had just said. It was going to take him a while to process all he was learning. He wondered if he was really up to the challenge. He knew that the only way to find out was to try.

"Yes, I'm going to do it," he said to Al.

Zeke looked out over the water. He noticed how peaceful it was. It reminded him of something else that he wanted to ask Al. "I have another question. Yesterday when I found you in the woods, you were meditating. I don't think that is something I can do because I live in the city. The only time I'm around woods, or water, or nature, is when we go camping or when we come to the farm. So what do I do about meditating?"

Al smiled. "Thank you, Zeke for reminding me about this," said Al. He chuckled as he continued. "The older I get the more forgetful I become at times. Here's some good news! You can meditate anywhere and anytime you want. Meditating is about relaxing the mind and body. So pick a quiet place…like your bedroom. Find a comfortable place to sit. When you're ready to begin meditating, take a deep breath and slowly exhale. When you feel your body start to relax, you should also relax your mind. This may be the hardest part. Usually many of us have so much on our minds and it's hard to let go of these distractions. I like visualizing a quiet stream of water or a field of beautiful lavender. Visualization is a powerful tool. Use it. And you must also think positive thoughts. I will explain more about this later."

"Have you ever wondered why it is that you dream when you are asleep?" continued Al.

"Never really thought about it, but now that you mention it, you're right! I never dream when I'm awake!"

"That's because when you are sleeping your mind is relaxed. A relaxed mind provides the path to connect to the universe. And, when you feel more comfortable with meditation, you can meditate with other people."

"No way," responded Zeke. "I'm not ready to tell my friends about what is happening."

"You don't have to, it's only a suggestion. I often meditate with a group of people."

"Why?" asked Zeke.

Al reached down and picked up a few small rocks from the ground. Then he asked Zeke to follow him. Al led Zeke to the water's edge. "Let me show you why." He handed Zeke a couple of the small rocks and ask him to throw one into the water.

Zeke did as he was asked. When the pebble hit the water, a few ripples broke the surface. "Perfect," said Al. "Did you notice the ripples that emanated from the impact of the rock on the water?"

"Yes," answered Zeke. "Dad taught us a long time ago how to skip stones across the water. It would be hard with this size rock, but if we found some small flat ones, they would skip really well. Skipping stones does the same thing."

Al grinned at Zeke's enthusiasm. Within a few minutes both of them found exactly what they were looking for. With the small flat rocks now in hand, Al continued with his lesson.

"You go first," said Al.

Zeke took a step back and positioned himself. After a few seconds he released his rock and watched it skip three times before it disappeared into the water.

Journey with Zeke

"Good one!" exclaimed Al.

"Thank you," responded Zeke humbly. "Now it's your turn."

Al released his rock and they both silently counted to five. "Wow!" said Zeke, "that was a really good skip."

Al again asked Zeke if he noticed the ripples. Zeke answered in the affirmative.

"Good. Now imagine those ripples representing a vibration that you send out to the universe. They watched as the ripples from the rocks cascaded out into the open water. Now I want you to imagine that you have five of your friends standing beside you and all of you skip your rocks at the same time."

Zeke immediately envisioned many ripples. "I get it," he exclaimed. "If each of those ripples represented the vibrations that we were sending to the universe, the universe would receive a bigger vibration."

"Yes! You are one extremely smart teenager," complimented Al. Do you realize that what you have learned in the past 48 hours is more than what many adults learn in a lifetime?"

Zeke blushed as he let the compliment sink in. Suddenly the look on Zeke's faced changed.

"That's why people pray together, isn't it?" questioned Zeke.

"Yes, son, it is. When people pray together they are sending a stronger message…a vibration to the universe. However, that doesn't mean that one prayer alone isn't heard, because it is."

Zeke felt a warm feeling come over him. He thought about the times that he had prayed alone and all the times that he had prayed with his family. He thought about when he had prayed at church. It wasn't until now that he truly understood how powerful prayer really was.

"Wow! I promise that when I feel more comfortable with it all, I will ask some of my friends to join me." Zeke couldn't wait to tell Griffen, his mom and dad everything that he had learned. He briefly wondered if his brother would give him a hard time like he had about his dreams, or if he would be more accepting now that they were both beginning to understand more about the universe and the mysteries it held.

"I accept that promise," said Al. "And I am always willing to pray or meditate with you anytime." Before Al could say anything further Zeke's phone rang and he quickly answered it. Al could tell by the way Zeke's face lit up that Dad had arrived. He watched Zeke's excitement as he ended the call.

"Can we go now? My dad's here," explained Zeke.

"Sure. You want to drive?" Al asked with a smile.

Zeke gave him a funny look back. "What kind of question is that?" He loved driving Old Bessie. He swiftly walked over to take his spot behind the wheel. "Hang on!" he yelled to Al, as he pressed down on the gas pedal.

Chapter 18

As they approached the farm, they saw Dad standing on the front porch. Zeke removed one hand from the steering wheel and started waving his arm wildly from side-to-side. He would have honked the horn to get his dad's attention, except that he didn't know if Old Bessie had a horn. Dad saw him waving and waved back.

Zeke brought the vehicle to a halt right in front of the steps. He jumped off and happily greeted his dad with a hug. Al stepped back and watched as the two reunited. Zeke introduced Al to his father. Jack reached out and shook Al's hand. "You have an amazing son," said Al.

"I couldn't agree more," replied Jack.

"So where is everybody?" questioned Zeke.

"Inside the nice cool house, which is right where we should be instead of out here in the heat," answered Dad as he opened the front porch door and held it until Zeke and Al were inside.

Zeke waited just inside the door and asked, "Hey, Dad, have you met Cat yet?"

"I sure have, Son."

Zeke led the way to the kitchen where everyone was seated at the kitchen table enjoying a cookie. Al, Zeke, and Dad each pulled out a chair to join them.

"You boys sure have been keeping yourselves busy, haven't you? Between chores, Barley, camping, fishing, Old Bessie, visiting Indian Burial grounds, and helping Grandpa with some special project, it's a wonder you have any energy left! I'm jealous," kidded their dad.

"We have been busy, Dad!" chirped Zeke. "Plus, we made two new friends."

Dad smiled as he looked at Cat and Al. "You can never have too many friends."

The group spent the rest of the afternoon sitting around the kitchen table chatting. "Do you think it's too hot for a fish fry?" asked Grandma.

"It's never too hot for fish!" exclaimed Grandpa.

Working as a team, they quickly set the table, including homemade tartar sauce and all the other fixings for their fish fry. Dad was a pro at frying fish. He had his own special batter and just as soon as the grease was hot enough he started dropping the fish into the fryer. The whole house quickly filled with the delicious aroma of frying fish. When the platter was filled with the golden morsels, they all sat down to enjoy them. Within thirty minutes the fish was gone. Al was the first to compliment Jack on his frying skills.

After dinner, everyone moved to the front porch to watch the sun set. Al purposely sat next to Jack. He was waiting for the right time to ask about helping Zeke understand his dreams, as well as mentoring him further with his spiritual abilities.

As the sun sank lower in the sky, the conversation slowly petered out. Griffen decided he was ready for a walk and asked Cat if she would like to join him. Cat was thrilled.

Barley was getting anxious and Zeke could tell he wanted to play. "Come on boy," he said as he patted the side of his leg. Barley was up and running. Zeke grabbed a stick that had been lying by the front porch and threw it far out in the yard for Barley to fetch.

Grandma announced that she was going to head back inside where it was cooler. Grandpa agreed that was a good idea. Jack stood up to join his parents. Al had been waiting for a moment like this and asked Jack if he would stay and chat with him for a moment.

Trying to put Jack at ease, he said, "You have amazing sons, Jack. You must be as proud of them as I am of my kids."

Journey with Zeke

"I am," replied Jack. "I sure did miss them this week while I was traveling. I'm not fond of being away from my family, but it's what my job requires. My parents said they understood why I moved away, but I'm not sure. My dad, being a farmer, was never away."

Al smiled. "I understand. You know Jack, your parents are very proud of you and even though we have never met face to face, I feel like I know you from the stories that I've heard about you."

Jack laughed. "I guess that's what happens when you become a parent. I'm guilty of that as well. I brag about my boys every chance I get. I've also heard about you, Al, and I'm surprised that we've only met today. My dad talks fondly of you and he told me about your wife passing away. I was so sorry to hear it. How have you been getting along?"

"It was extremely hard at first, not being able to see her in person everyday. But I know in my heart and my mind that she is happy and doing well. You know, Jack, some people don't believe what I'm about to say, so I hope that I don't shock you. My wife comes to visit me in my dreams. It's only happened a few times, but I treasure those times." Al studied Jack's face as he waited for Jack to respond.

Jack turned his head to look at the ground. "I'm sure it's been hard. I can't even imagine it. I've never lost someone that was so close to me."

Al could tell that Jack was getting a little uncomfortable with the direction the conversation was taking. He thought now was the time to ask for Jack's permission to mentor Zeke and help him understand his dreams. He proceeded with caution.

"I want to ask you something, Jack. During our camping trip with George and your sons, Zeke shared with me a dream that he's been having about your dad. He also said that an Indian lady by the name of Moon Willow has been appearing in these dreams."

Jack jerked his head up and looked directly at Al. "Yes, I'm aware of his dreams," he snipped. "It's like you said, Al, he's an amazing kid with a great imagination. I wouldn't worry about what he's told you. He's fine and I'm sure that he'll outgrow this phase. I think some of it got started with Griffen's ghost stories. They scare Zeke sometimes, and I think it's his way of coping."

Al knew that he had to try to convince Jack that the dreams were more than a coping mechanism. Pressing on, he said, "I believe what Zeke has told me, Jack. I believe in spirit guides. I am a Hopi Indian descendant. My great-great grandfather was a well-known medicine man. I have been taught, just like the generations before me, that everyone has a spirit guide. They are always with us. In Zeke's case, he has the ability to communicate with his spirit guide because he is open to listening. However, I'm concerned that he lacks the understanding of what to do with the messages that he receives in his dreams. With your permission, I would like to offer my help. I'm more than willing to mentor your son, so that he can continue to grow and develop his spiritual ability."

Jack hesitated for a moment. "I appreciate your offer, Al, but you live here and we live pretty far away." Jack felt this was the safest way to get out of this situation. He didn't want to offend Al. After all, he knew how much his dad thought of him, but he really didn't like the idea of a virtual stranger playing a role in his son's life and filling his head with crazy ideas.

"That won't be a problem, Jack. With today's technology it's easier than ever to stay in touch. Cat is a whiz at technology and she helps me a lot."

Jack was a good negotiator. He often used this technique at work. He didn't want to come right out and say no. He could feel that Al believed in the offer he was making. Yet, he did not want his son's head filled with beliefs that he wasn't sure he believed himself. "Let's do this," replied Jack. "I promise to call you if Zeke continues to have dreams and I see that he is struggling with them."

Al knew the conversation had come to end. He nodded in agreement. "Fair enough, Jack. My offer stands and you can call me any time."

Jack stood up. "I'm going to go inside where it's cooler and relax a bit with my parents. You want to join me?"

"Sure, in a few minutes. I'm going to wait here until Cat returns. I'm sure she'll be back soon."

"Okay, see you inside," said Jack, heading for the front door.

Journey with Zeke

Zeke noticed that his dad had gone inside. With Barley at his side, he ran up to the front porch and sat down next to Al. "Did you get to ask him?"

"Yes, Zeke, I did."

"What did he say?"

Al thought for a minute about telling Zeke that his dad didn't go for it, but that he should go ahead and contact him anyway. But he didn't want to mar the budding relationship with deceit. He was honest with Zeke and respected his father's wishes. "Your dad said that if you continued to have the dreams and needed help, he would contact me and let me know."

Zeke nodded his head in acknowledgement. He could tell that Al was disappointed. "Ah, it's okay, Al. Moon Willow told me that he would resist at first. If it is meant to be, it will be, right?"

Al chuckled. "Right, Zeke. You are one smart young man."

"Cool. Look, here comes Griffen and Cat. I'm going to run out and meet them." Al stayed on the porch and watched as Zeke and Barley ran down the driveway to meet the young couple. When they returned to the porch, Al told his granddaughter that it was time for them to head home. He wanted the Cook family to enjoy some private time and he did not want to overstay their welcome.

"Okay, Granddad," replied Cat. "I'll go inside and get my purse." Everyone followed Cat inside. Once Cat had retrieved her purse, she and Granddad thanked everyone for their hospitality, the camping trip, and the fish fry.

Griffen and Zeke walked them to the car. Cat made the 'phone me' sign to Griffen as they were driving away. Griffen wondered how long he should wait before he called her. He felt like he wanted to call right then, but their car wasn't even out of the driveway yet.

Back in the house, the boys, their dad, and grandparents spent the rest of the evening chatting, joking and catching-up. Mom called and each of them spoke to her, relaying their version of what had happened in the last couple of days. She filled them in one by one about Grandma B and how she was feeling better.

Zeke was the first to notice how late it was getting. He was exhausted and Barley was already fast asleep at his feet. "I'm going to bed," he announced.

"Will you let Barley out first?" asked his grandpa.

"Sure," replied Zeke. "Come on, boy, let's go outside." Barley jumped up and followed Zeke to the back door. A few minutes later, Zeke and Barley were in bed. Zeke was excited about going home. He had a fun time here, but was ready to see his friends again. School would be starting soon and there were things at home he still wanted to do. Within seconds, he was asleep.

Chapter 19

ZEKE WAS GETTING USED TO seeing Moon Willow in his dreams. He listened to her and was learning not to be afraid of what she was showing him. As he relaxed and became more comfortable, he found that he wasn't afraid anymore. He never knew for sure how she was going to appear. That made his dreams more interesting. He wondered if his mood had anything to do with how and when she appeared.

Once again he heard Moon Willow's voice, but this time he did not see her. He listened as he heard her say, "I need to show you something."

He waited in the darkness of his dream, noticing a brilliant white light that was off in the distance. "Where is she?" he thought to himself.

"I'm right here, Zeke," came the answer from Moon Willow.

"You were right about Dad. Al talked to him and he resisted."

"It will be okay, Zeke. Al will be there for you when you need him," she reassured him.

"I know," responded Zeke.

"Zeke, before I show you what I need to show you, I want you to understand that you will not always be shown this much detail about events or circumstances. I have shared more than I usually do. From this point on you will be on a 'need to know basis' as they say. You must learn to listen with an open mind, and recognize that there are many different levels at which we will communicate with you."

"Okay," replied Zeke. In an instant, they were standing outside the man cave door to the barn. Zeke smiled because he knew that this was Grandpa's home away from home.

Moon Willow magically appeared next to Zeke. Without another word she began to float away. It was like watching a balloon being released and watching it until you could no longer see it. Zeke was puzzled. She had never done anything like this before. She sure was full of surprises. He found it amusing in a way, that she was capable of doing everything she did. He waited patiently for something to happen. It felt like he stood there forever.

A feeling came over him that he should open the barn door to the man cave. He did, but no one was inside. He continued to wait. Suddenly he saw dark shadows developing around him. Normally he would have run away, but this time he didn't. Instead he thought, "There is no reason to be afraid. Stay put and see what happens next."

Even though he could not see their faces, he began to feel like he knew who they were. An ambulance appeared with its lights flashing. He saw the letter "G" float by. It was surrounded by a huge heart that looked like a valentine heart. The numbers 911 appeared in white on the front of the red barn door. It reminded him an address on the front of a house, but he knew that barns didn't have addresses.

One of the dark forms began changing from its dark color. He watched as the form turned into an image of his dad. He was kneeling on the ground, but Zeke couldn't see what it was he was doing.

He could hear a phone ringing in the background. Turning around to see where the ringing was coming from, he saw a cell phone hanging in the air all by itself. Thinking the call was for him, he reached up and grabbed the cell phone and said "Hello?" The voice on the other end simply said, "What will be is meant to be." It was a voice he did not recognize.

Then he felt himself being pulled. He didn't want to leave. He wanted to stay and see what else would appear in his dream, but the pull was too strong.

Chapter 20

Zeke slowly opened his eyes and saw his brother looking down at him. "Come on Zeke, get up. You've got to get packed. Dad wants to leave within the hour," Griffen said.

Zeke let out a yawn while he stretched. Not yet motivated to actually get out of bed, he started watching Griffen pack his duffle bag. "You better get up, Zeke," repeated Griffen gruffly.

"I am," snapped Zeke, and then quickly added, "You're sure grumpy this morning. I'll be packed before you are, so don't worry about it."

Zeke jumped out of bed and quickly changed his clothes. What Griffen didn't know was that he had packed the day before, so once he added his pj's, he was officially packed. He couldn't help himself as he walked past his brother. "You better hurry, Griffen, you're going to be late for breakfast," he smirked.

Griffen picked up a pair of dirty socks off the floor and threw them at his brother. Zeke ducked and the socks flew over the top of his head. Laughing, he left the socks where they landed and took off running down the stairs. All he had left was to put on his shoes, but they were by the back door. As Zeke entered the kitchen, he said good morning to his grandparents and Dad. "Where's Griffen?" asked Dad.

"Oh, you mean slow poke?" answered Zeke. "He's still packing."

"No, I'm not. I'm right here, Zekey Boy," quipped Griffen, as he entered the kitchen. Zeke turned around and gave his brother a dirty look. The brothers' old habits kicked in as they prepared to return home.

"Okay, boys, that's enough," said Dad. "We have a long drive ahead of us, and I'm not going to listen to this all day."

Zeke grabbed his shoes and went to the table. Griffen threw down his duffle bag and slouched down at the table as well. He didn't want to leave Cat.

There was an eerie silence at breakfast. Zeke wasn't sure why everyone was being so quiet. He ate his breakfast while furtively sneaking glances at everyone.

Toward the end of breakfast, Grandpa was the first to break the silence. "Hey, Jack, do you remember the old box car that you and I built when you were about 12 years old?"

"I sure do. I loved that car!"

"I've got a special surprise for you. I found it out in the barn not too long ago. Yesterday, Cat and Griffen helped put on the finishing touches. I want you to have it. Stay here, I'm going to get it for you."

Grandpa stood up slowly. He didn't seem to be himself this morning. Jack figured that the boys being there all week had worn him out. He certainly understood that teenage boys could be a handful.

Grandma looked concerned as she watched her husband stand. He didn't usually move that slowly. She wondered if the camping, fishing, chores and everything else was catching up to him. They had been married almost fifty years and she knew that he had a hard time relaxing. Normally she would have questioned him right then and there, but with everyone else sitting at the table, and knowing that her husband disliked being put on the spot, she decided she would wait until after all the company had left.

As Grandpa reached the door, he did the best imitation he could of one of his favorite actors. Everyone laughed when they heard him say, "I'll be back." Jack laughed the loudest just as he had all those years ago when his father first tried imitating the famous actor. They had watched "The Terminator" many times together. It was a fond memory.

Everyone else started clearing the table. Jack kept waiting for his dad to return. He was really excited about seeing his car again. It held some fond memories. During the clean up he asked his mother how his father had been feeling lately. He knew that Zeke had a dream about him, not that he believed in those types of dreams. Outside of that, neither his father nor mother had mentioned how they had been feeling. Whenever he asked, they would say the same thing - "a little ache here and a little pain there, nothing out of the ordinary for someone my age."

Grandma assured Jack that George had been feeling well, and then commented that she, too, had noticed that he was moving a bit slower than usual that morning.

Finally Jack couldn't take it any longer. He didn't want to rush his dad, but he wanted to get on the road early so they would be home by dark. Plus, he was a little concerned about what could be taking him so long. He let everyone know that he was going to go to the barn.

"Let's all go, Jack," replied his mother. "I know your father is proud and I can't wait to see how your old box car turned out. I'm sure he's checking it over twice to make sure it's perfect."

"I bet you're right, Mom. I remember winning my one and only blue ribbon with that box car." Everyone laughed.

They all walked together toward the barn and the boys listened to Grandma and Dad talk about the day he had won his blue ribbon. "Grandpa and I worked two weeks prior to the race getting the car ready. It had to be sanded just right. We had decided on painting the car red, white, and blue. We added the number 12 as the car's number because that was how old I was at the time."

Zeke was the first to see him. Grandpa was lying on the ground by the barn door of the man cave. With lightning speed, Zeke took off running. As soon as he reached him he dropped to his knees. Dad arrived right behind him. He yelled for Zeke to move out of the way. Zeke jumped back as Dad knelt down and checked for a pulse. It's what his dad yelled next that shook everyone to the core. "I can't find a pulse!"

"Griffin…call 911! Grandpa's having a heart attack!" yelled his dad, as he started CPR.

Zeke saw tears running down Grandma's face. She knelt down and held Grandpa's hand as she pleaded, "Stay with us George. Stay with us!"

Griffen quickly called 911. He put his phone on speaker so Dad and Grandma could hear the dispatcher. "Does anyone know CPR?" asked the level-headed dispatcher on the other end of the phone. Griffen explained that his dad had already started CPR.

"The ambulance is on its way. I'm going to stay on the line with you until they get there," said the dispatcher. "Keep giving CPR."

It seemed like it took forever for the ambulance to arrive. With the siren blaring they entered the driveway. As soon as they came to a stop, both paramedics jumped out and headed to the man that was lying on the ground. Everyone moved out of the way so the paramedics could take over. The family watched as the paramedics took his vitals and shocked his chest three times. Finally, on the third try, they announced that there was a light heartbeat. The paramedics did a few other things and then quickly loaded him into the ambulance. They left in a blur with the siren once again blaring.

As the ambulance pulled out of the driveway, Dad ran to get his truck. He told the boys to stay and that he would call them as soon as he could, as he helped his mom into the passenger side of the truck. Moving quickly, he ran to the driver's side and jumped in.

The boys did not argue with their dad. Stunned by everything that had just happened, they stood in the driveway and watched as Dad and Grandma sped away. It took a few minutes before either of them moved. Griffen turned to his brother with a bewildered look on his face. "What … just … happened?" he muttered slowly, stuttering in shock.

Zeke started crying. He leaned onto Griffen's arm, gripping it tightly. Through the sobs, he exclaimed, "I think Grandpa had a heart attack."

"I think he did, too. That's what Dad said at least," said Griffen. "Grandpa should have listened to you. After all, you had the dreams. You told him to go to the doctor, but would he listen? No! And now this! I am so angry! What happens if he dies, Zeke?"

Zeke shook his head. He didn't want to think about Grandpa dying. At breakfast he had decided not to share the dream he had the night before. He was feeling very guilty about that decision. He blurted, "I had another dream last night."

"No way," responded Griffen. "What happened in your dream? Did Grandpa die?"

"I don't know. The dream wasn't like any of the past ones. Moon Willow took me to the barn door and then she floated away like a balloon until I couldn't see her anymore. After that I saw an ambulance. I saw Dad doing something on the ground, but I couldn't see what. I also saw 911 in white letters on the barn door to Grandpa's man cave."

"You didn't see Grandpa anywhere in this dream?" quizzed Griffen.

"No, I didn't. I know now that the dream was about Grandpa, but I didn't know this morning when I woke up. I'm sorry."

"Don't be sorry," reassured Griffen. "This is not your fault."

"I know, but I don't understand why Moon Willow would show me everything she did and then not show me whether or not Grandpa will live. I don't think that's fair. I want to know. You want to know." Zeke suddenly started screaming up at the sky. "Why? I hate this, Griffen! I hate this! Al said that what I had was a gift. It sure doesn't feel like a gift today. It feels like a curse!"

Griffen put his arms around his screaming brother. "It's not your fault, Zeke." Griffen felt torn up inside. None of this felt fair, but he knew Zeke did not cause the heart attack.

"I know it's not my fault," cried Zeke. "All I know is that I hate Moon Willow. I wish she would go away and leave me alone!"

Griffen didn't like seeing his brother so upset. He, too, was really upset and he certainly didn't understand why anyone would have to endure the type of dreams that Zeke had been having. Feeling confused, angry and alone, he called Mom to let her know what had just happened.

Mom consoled both her sons as best she could for being thousands of miles away. They could tell from her voice that she was also crying. She suggested that Griffen call Al and ask that he and Cat come and be with them so that they weren't alone while waiting to hear from their dad. She was worried about them witnessing such a terrible ordeal. She was going to try to reach Dad at the hospital.

As soon as Griffen hung up, he texted Cat to let her know what had happened. He was going to ask if she and Al would come over, but before he could, Cat sent back a text that said, "BRT." Griffen knew the acronym meant they would "be right there".

Griffen told Zeke that Cat and Al were on their way. He would try to take on the care-giving role the best he could and look out for his little brother. "Let's go and sit on the porch and wait for them," he suggested. Still crying, Zeke followed his brother to the porch and sat down beside him on the swing. Barley followed and lay down at Zeke's feet. As they sat on the porch swing Zeke slowly ran his feet through Barley's fur. Neither brother spoke. Silently, they waited.

When Al and Cat arrived, Griffen somberly filled them in on everything that had happened. Al asked Griffen and Zeke if they were okay. Zeke nodded his head yes, but he was not sure that he meant it. His eyes were puffy from crying.

Griffen felt his phone vibrate. "It's Dad!" He quickly read the text message to everyone.

Dad: *At hospital U ok?*

Griffen: *yes*

Dad: *Zeke ok?*

Griffen: *yes. Al Cat r here*

Dad: *Good ask them to stay plz.*

Griffen: *k called mom*

Dad: *talked to her 2*

Dad: *No news yet. Love u*

Griffen: *lu2 Dad*

Griffen closed his phone and sat in silence. Cat walked over to him. "I'm sorry about your grandpa," she said looking at Griffen and then at Zeke. Griffen smiled slightly. Just having her by his side made him feel a little bit better.

Griffen looked at his brother. "Tell Al about the dream."

Zeke put his face in his hands and started crying again. Everyone waited. They didn't want to push. When he finally spoke he could barely muster the words. Through the sobs, he stated, "I had a terrible dream

Journey with Zeke

last night about Grandpa." Looking up, he saw everyone looking at him, waiting to hear what he was going to say.

Al could see and feel Zeke's sadness. He told Zeke to take a deep breath and to try and relax.

Zeke sat up straight, closed his eyes and took a deep breath. He exhaled slowly. Listening to Al's instructions, he took another deep breath and slowly released it. Zeke could feel his body beginning to relax a little. He took another deep breath and slowly released again.

"Good," said Al. "You're doing a good job."

As his body relaxed, Zeke was able to gain control of his crying. He began again to relay the details of his dream. "In my dream I saw Dad kneeling on the ground, the same way I saw him today. I didn't know that it was Grandpa lying by the barn door. I saw the ambulance and 911 in white letters on the barn door. If Moon Willow had showed me more, I could have insisted that Grandpa go directly to the hospital, instead of out to the barn." When he was finished, he took another deep breath and waited for someone to respond.

"Zeke, you had what is called a protection dream," began Al. "When we are open to accepting guidance from our spirit guide, you can receive messages like those you have been receiving in your dreams. Each experience can be different. I have had those types of dreams, too."

"Me, too, Zeke," said Cat. "A couple of nights before my grandmother passed away, I had a dream about her. In that dream, I saw her surrounded by angel wings. My spirit guide, Peter, was standing by her bed. I remember Peter telling me that it was almost time for my grandmother to come home. She had been in a coma for a couple of days. Peter said my grandmother's family and friends in the spirit world were gathering to greet her when she crossed over from the Earth plane to the Spiritual plane. He asked me to gather family and friends around her here, too.

"When I woke that morning, I was really shaken. I went to Granddad immediately and told him about my dream." Looking lovingly at her granddad, she continued, "Granddad told me that my spirit guide was preparing me, and that we should do exactly what he had asked, so we did. For the next few days, our house was continually filled with family and friends. When Grandmother died, I know in my heart and in my mind that she was surrounded by much love."

Zeke saw the tears swelling in Cat's eyes. He went over to her and gave her hug. She hugged him back. "I know that Grandmother is in heaven." As Zeke backed away from her, Cat touched her heart and said, "And she is with me every day in spirit."

Zeke looked at Al. "Did you dream the same dream?" he asked.

"No, Zeke, I didn't. As you know, I have had many similar dreams about other family members, friends and even people I don't know, but I did not have a dream about my wife."

"Why? I don't understand," pushed Zeke.

"I believe the message was delivered to Cat for a reason. I was very emotional at the time and wasn't able to receive messages very well. That's not to say that my spirit guide didn't try. I was just not open to receive a message."

Griffen had been listening intently to the conversation, so much so that when his phone rang it caused him to jump. He grabbed his phone and recognized his mom's number.

"Hi, Mom," he answered. Griffen spoke to his mom for a little bit and then handed the phone to Zeke. Zeke wanted to be brave for his mom, and was determined not to cry while she was on the phone. He listened for a second or two and suddenly his face lit up with a smile. Whatever she said sure had made him happy. Zeke finished talking with his mom and handed the phone back to Griffen, as he excitedly announced. "Mom's flying out later today. She'll be here tonight!"

"Yes!" exclaimed Griffen. Knowing that their mom would be coming home was all it took to help change the brothers' mood. They were still worried about Grandpa, but somehow knowing that Mom was coming helped serve as a distraction from their anguish and redirected their thoughts. "I'll bet she'll be exhausted when she gets here. Why don't we go inside and figure out something for dinner tonight?"

Everyone agreed. Now that they had something to occupy their hands and their minds, the afternoon flew by.

Journey with Zeke

Griffen heard the grandfather clock in the living room chime three times. "Wow!" he thought, "I wonder why I haven't heard anything from Dad?" For a split second, he thought about calling him, but then thought better of it. Dad said he would let them know later in the day how Grandpa was doing. Griffen would have to be patient and let that happen.

Thirty minutes later, Griffen's phone rang. He answered and put it on speaker so they could all listen. Dad told them Grandpa had had a heart attack. He explained that Grandpa had two blocked arteries and some other stuff going on with his heart that would require him to have open heart surgery. The surgeon had been called in to do the emergency surgery. Dad and Grandma would be staying at the hospital until the surgery was completed.

The boys let him know that Mom had called and they were really excited about her coming to the farm. Dad said he had talked with her also and that her plane would be landing at 4:00 p.m. that day. She would be coming to the hospital first and then she would be on her way to see them.

Just as they were getting ready to hang up, Zeke hollered, "Dad, we made a bunch of food so don't worry about us and dinner!"

"Thanks, Zeke," replied his dad. "I'm sure it's all delicious." Dad's laughter, over the phone, was a nice sound to hear.

"Hey, Buddy," continued Dad, "would you please take the phone off speaker and hand the phone to Al?"

"Will do. He's standing right here, Dad. Love you!" Zeke took the phone off speaker and handed it to Al.

With the phone in hand, Al walked into the next room. Since Jack had asked for the phone to be taken off speaker, Al assumed that he wanted to talk in private. Their conversation lasted for almost ten minutes.

When Al reappeared in the kitchen, he asked all of them to come and sit down at the kitchen table. He looked directly at Griffen and Zeke. "You both know I was just speaking with your dad. He has given me permission to guide both of you."

"Your dad said he felt it was important for you to be able to talk about what you have been experiencing with the dreams and the messages. Griffen, I know that you and I have not spent a lot of time together, but I would like to mentor you and help you understand the voices that you have been hearing. I hope you don't mind that Cat told me. I would like to help you understand that the voices you are hearing are a form of communication from the spirit world. "

Griffen smiled at Cat, who was looking at him and awaiting his response. Then he smiled at Al. "I don't mind at all. I guess it's something I should get used to and understand. I just hope it's not like Zeke."

Al smiled back. "I explained to your dad that my life-long experiences will help to guide you both in many ways. I have shared a little bit of knowledge and so has Cat, but there is so much more to learn about dreams, visits, meditation, and energy."

"Really?" exclaimed Zeke. "Like what?"

"Oh gosh, let's see. Our destiny, life-path, life lessons, energy vibrations… I could go on and on. For now, have Cat show you the Facebook page she created for you Zeke."

Zeke unpacked his laptop. A few minutes later Cat had shown everyone the page she had created. She had titled the page "JourneywithZeke." Seeing the pleased look on Zeke's face she encouraged him to get busy. "The rest is up to you, my friend. Text your friends and tell them to look for your Facebook page."

Zeke said "Thanks!" and challenged his brother to see who could get more friends to "Like" their page.

"You're on," replied Griffen.

Griffen immediately started texting his friends. "I'm in a contest against my brother and I want to win. Just type my name in the comment section, and it will be counted as a vote for me." He was happy for his brother and proud of the page that Cat had designed. To him she titled the page perfectly. He understood that both of them were on a journey, but having a page dedicated to his brother felt good.

Not wanting to be outdone by his brother, Zeke sent out his own message titled, "Freaky Dreams" and provided the same information that Griffen had.

Replies to Zeke's texts started immediately.

Jimmy: *Hey bro, you go off the deep end?*

Tim: *like it?*

Dustin: *You crack me up!*

Perry: *Going there now!*

Jason: *When you coming back?*

Dom: *lol*

Sherry: *Sounds interesting!*

Sam: *Cool!*

Sarah: *What's up!*

Jude: *Got ya!*

Kristy: *did u go on vacation?*

Griffen's friends were also texting him. This project would hopefully help their friends understand instead of thinking they were weird.

At 9:00 p.m., Griffen's phone rang. It was Dad. Once again he put his phone on speaker so everyone could listen. "Grandpa is out of surgery. They will be moving him to his own room in a little while. He's doing as well as can be expected. We'll know more in the morning. Mom arrived safely and is here with us. She's anxious to see you both. Grandma wants to stay at the hospital tonight with Grandpa. Mom and I are going to stay, too. Is that okay with you guys?"

Everyone said it was okay. Secretly, Zeke wished they would come home, but he kept it to himself.

Al reminded their dad that he and Cat were prepared to stay for as long as they were needed. "Don't worry about a thing. We're here. Just call if you need anything."

After they had hung up, Al suggested that everyone head to the kitchen for a snack. Without hesitation they agreed. They each grabbed a cookie and some milk. While they were enjoying the snack, everyone joked about who would win the contest between Griffen and Zeke. Cat asked Granddad who he thought would win. Not wanting to take sides, Al simply replied, "It will be what it is meant to be." The boys both chuckled. Then Al added, "I think it's time for bed," as he yawned for the third time. "We've got a lot of chores to do in the morning and we have to get up early."

Griffen gathered pillows and blankets for Cat and Al. Thirty minutes later, their guests were asleep in the living room. Upstairs, the boys chatted a bit as they tried to fall asleep. Zeke reminded Griffen to say his prayers for Grandpa and for Grandma B. Griffen answered, "I already have."

Chapter 21

Zeke saw Grandpa lying in a hospital bed with his eyes closed. From the doorway of the hospital room, he took quick notice of a machine with a red squiggly line that would jump up to a point and then down and wondered what its purpose was. He also noticed the tubes running from clear bags of fluid that connected to him.

Happy to see him and wanting to let his grandpa know that he had been really worried, he took two steps toward the bed, but was stopped. When he tried again, the same thing happened. It was as if an invisible wall prevented him from going any further. It reminded Zeke of the dreams where he had seen Grandpa lying in the casket at the church – the dreams he had once called nightmares.

Not understanding why he was being blocked, he looked around the room to see if there was another way to move closer. It was hard to see. The room was dark with the exception of a dim night light. There was also a little light coming in from the hallway. With his eyes, he slowly began searching the room. On the right side of the room he noticed a small ball of white light hovering above a chair. Normally, he wouldn't have paid much attention to this and would have missed it. However, if there was one thing he had learned since meeting Moon Willow, it was that she could appear anytime, anywhere and in any form, and little balls of light should not be dismissed.

Moon Willow had told him that when he saw a light ball that he was actually seeing an orb. Orbs were the energy form that allowed spirits to move quickly from one place to another. That was exactly what this orb was doing. It was moving very rapidly around the room. He could see it one second, and the next second it was gone, only to reappear again in a different part of the room. It reminded him of the golden snitch from Harry Potter, darting all over. He watched the orb as it jetted over to Grandpa and then it came directly at him.

Watching the orb float, hover, disappear and reappear, made him chuckle. He didn't feel any fear whatsoever. In fact, watching it also reminded him of a particular part in a movie that he had seen several times called "The Wizard of Oz." He enjoyed all the characters in the movie, but what he was seeing now reminded him of the part where Glinda the Good Witch had floated in a bubble; a bubble that had started out small. It was magical the way she had landed in Munchkin Land. It reminded him of Moon Willow as she either magically appeared or floated in from some far away place.

Hearing a familiar voice, he turned his head to the right and there stood Moon Willow. This time she was not alone. Floating next to her was a red-haired man, who looked to be somewhat younger than Moon Willow. He generated the same warmth and love that Moon Willow did.

"Hi Zeke," said Moon Willow. "I want to introduce you to Robert." Before Zeke could acknowledge Robert, Moon Willow continued speaking. "Any second now your grandpa's spirit is going to rise up out of his body. Robert, who is your grandpa's spirit guide, is here to make sure everything goes the way it is supposed to."

In that instant an alarm started ringing. Zeke turned and realized the alarm was coming from the machine that was connected to Grandpa. The red line that had been going up and down was now a straight red line moving across the monitor. In short order, there were several people in the now brightly lit hospital room. They surrounded the bed. Each appeared to be doing something different, yet he sensed that they were working as a team. He watched as a man in a long white coat rubbed two paddles together and yelled, "Clear!"

Suddenly a brilliant white light appeared in the room. No one seemed to care that it was there, and that puzzled Zeke. Moon Willow immediately answered his question, even though he had not asked one aloud. "No one else in the room can see the white light except for us and your grandpa.

Journey with Zeke

Zeke, the white light is how spirits transition from the earth's plane to the spiritual plane.

Zeke was stunned. "Are you telling me that Grandpa just died?"

"Yes, Zeke, I am," answered Moon Willow.

"I don't understand. I should be crying because Grandpa just died. Instead, all I feel is happiness for him. There is such warmth, love, and happiness coming from that white light and from the two of you. Look - there are dark shadows standing in the white light! Who are they?" Zeke wasn't sure if he was supposed to feel excited or scared since he had never experienced anything like this before.

Moon Willow explained, in a reassuring voice, that they were family and friends gathering to greet his grandpa as he journeyed home.

"I'm hearing another voice," said Zeke. She says her name is Evelyn and she wants me to give a message to Al and Cat. She wants me to tell them that she loves them very much and that she is holding a bouquet of red roses.

Moon Willow and Robert nodded that they understood. Moon Willow continued with her teaching. "Then that is what you must do, Zeke, deliver the message to them. It is part of your gift. It is a part of your destiny while you live on the earth's plane. You will help others understand what might seem impossible to understand. We are all on a spiritual journey, and at birth our minds are cleared and we forget that we have come to the earth's plane to learn life's lessons and grow spiritually.

As you grow older and become more comfortable with your gift, you will connect many loved ones together from both planes, bringing them peace and comfort knowing that they are all okay."

Robert moved forward and quietly said to Zeke, "You should watch what is about to happen," as he pointed to Zeke's grandpa. Zeke turned to look and saw Grandpa's spirit rise out of his body and go into the white light. Zeke was moved and awestruck by what he had just seen. "It's amazing!" he exclaimed.

"Hold on Zeke. It's not your grandpa's time yet," said Robert.

Turning toward Robert, Zeke asked, "What do you mean?"

Robert pointed back to the hospital bed. Zeke turned back just as he heard the man in the white coat say, "We've got a heartbeat." The red line on the machine started moving up and down again. Everyone in the room had a look of relief on their faces. Zeke heard one nurse say to another, "We saved another one." The girl she was talking too said, "You're right, Beth."

Zeke stood in awe. "You mean Grandpa didn't die?"

"No, he didn't," replied Moon Willow. "As Robert said, it wasn't his time. Be blessed as you continue on your spiritual journey. By the way, Grandma B is going to be with you for a long time yet, also. It's time for us to go now."

Chapter 22

ZEKE WOKE UP TO THE morning alarm of Bud the rooster doing his usual cock-a-doodle-doo. Rolling over, he saw that Griffen wasn't in bed and Barley wasn't there either. He couldn't wait another second to tell everyone about his dream. Jumping out of bed he raced for the stairs. When he entered the kitchen, Al, Cat, and Griffen were sitting at the kitchen table, as well Dad and Mom. Barley sat at Griffen's feet.

He ran to his mother and gave her a big hug and then gave one to his dad. They both looked exhausted, but Zeke couldn't wait another second. Exhilarated by his dream, he quickly announced, "I had the most awesome dream last night!"

"Zeke," interrupted Dad. "Before you tell us about your dream, let me finish telling everyone about Grandpa."

"I already know," responded Zeke. "He's doing great. It isn't his time. His heart quit beating again and they had to revive him, but he's going to be okay." He went on to tell them about the man in a long white coat, and about a nurse named Beth. And how a brilliant white light had appeared in Grandpa's room and there were family and friends that looked like dark shadows that appeared in the white light. That these family and friends were waiting for Grandpa. He had seen Grandpa's spirit rise up out of his body and go to the white light and just as quickly his spirit had returned to his body. That was when he heard the man in the long white coat say, 'We got a heartbeat.'"

Nobody said a word. Zeke's parents looked stunned. Zeke was smiling from ear to ear as he moved around the kitchen table to stand next to Al and Cat. "There was a lady in my dream. She said her name was

Evelyn. She wanted me to tell you both that she loves you very much and that she was holding a bouquet of red roses.

"Okay, that's it!" said a beaming Zeke. "That's everything that I dreamed last night, and I have to add, I'm not afraid of my dreams anymore." Looking at Al he said, "You were right. It was a protection dream. Moon Willow was preparing me for when Grandpa had his heart attack, and even though I didn't dream about Grandma B, she let me know that she was going to be okay, too."

Al stood and gave Zeke a hug. He had tears running down his cheeks. "Zeke you are absolutely amazing. You didn't know this, because I never told you, but my wife's name is Evelyn. Thank you, son, for sharing her message with us." Cat also gave Zeke a hug and smiled through teary eyes.

Dad and Mom sat in their chairs trying to comprehend what they had just heard. Everything that Zeke had just said was what had happened during the night. They had been told that the heart surgery had saved Grandpa's life. There would be a recovery time and then he would be able to return to his daily routine.

Mom was the one who was the most surprised. She had only been gone for a week. She had talked to her sons on the phone, but they never told her about Zeke's continuous dreams. She vaguely recalled Griffen mentioning that he was going to throw the willow sticks away. She had laughed to herself when Griffen mentioned that they had some kind of mystical power and he thought that it was making him and his brother crazy. Somehow, somewhere, something had changed. She had never met Al or Cat, even though she had heard a lot of nice things about them. Placing her arm on the table, she turned to her husband and asked him to pinch her.

"What?" laughed Jack.

"Pinch me," repeated his wife. "I want to make sure I'm not dreaming or something. I know I'm tired, but all of this is a little bit weird first thing in the morning."

Griffen jumped up and ran around the table to his mom. "You're not dreaming, Mom. Yes, you're tired, but all of this is real, including Zeke's dreams. And get this – I also hear spirits, and I'm not afraid of being made fun of anymore!"

Wanting to be funny, Mom joked, "but I thought you threw the willow sticks away."

Griffen laughed, "Mom, we really do need to catch you up."

"Tell you what, Honey," said Dad to his wife, "let's get something to eat and I will fill you in on our amazing sons and the special gifts that they have. These gifts are going to help many people and have turned me into a believer of dreams and the blessings that come with them."

As they sat down to a breakfast of blueberry pancakes, they all joined hands in prayer. Each took a turn to say out loud what they were thankful for. At the end of their prayer they said in unison, "Amen."

"Now let's eat!" said Zeke.

About the Author

WHEN I WAS FOUR YEARS old, my family lived in the Upper Peninsula of Michigan. My father worked as a telephone contractor, and we traveled for his work. My parents rented an old farm house that was located a half mile off the main road. It was beautiful. To this day I remember the two-story, white, painted house, the red barns, and the slope of the back yard that led down to a beautiful stream where a solitary bridge had been built to allow one to cross to the other side.

Late one spring night we received a horrible thunderstorm. You know, the really scary kind - where the lightning lights up the entire sky as it streaks down in sharp jagged points in several different directions. The thunder was so loud that night that it boomed and left behind an echo that kept the windows shaking. I could hear the wind howling and wondered if it would blow our house away. Of course, I'm exaggerating, but not by much.

My twin sister and I shared a bedroom on the second story of the old farmhouse. It was located directly across the hall from my parents' room. My bed was positioned so that I could look out of our bedroom door and into my parents' bedroom and right out of their double-sash window.

I was wakened by the booming thunder and quickly realized that the electricity was out because our night light wasn't on. It was pitch black in our room and in my parents' room. I was scared.

As I lay wide awake in fear, I turned to face the window in my parent's room. I kept my eyes closed and when the thunder was really loud, I even covered my head with the blanket. Then all seemed too quiet. I removed the blanket from my head and looked across the hall and out of the window.

That's when it all happened. There was a bright lightning streak that lit up the sky, and that's when I saw it. A dark figure stepped through my parents' second story bedroom window.

I froze! I could not believe what I was seeing! I closed my eyes, and then I opened them again. As I adjusted once again to the blackness of the room I saw that the dark figure was slowly heading toward our bedroom doorway. It looked like it was floating toward me in really slow motion.

I wanted to scream, but nothing came out. I quickly covered my head again with my blanket. A couple of seconds later, I very slowly uncovered my eyes. The dark figure was still floating toward our doorway. I watched as it reached the center of the bedroom. Then it stopped.

I remember clearly thinking, "What is this thing doing in our room?"

Next, I heard a voice that said, "Don't be afraid."

I didn't listen. I was scared to death! I responded by yelling, "Go away!"

I covered up my head again and waited for what seemed like an eternity, but I am sure it was only a couple of seconds. Curious to see if it was still there, I once again uncovered my head.

Another lightning bolt lit up the room. It was still there!

I crawled out of my bed. All I could think was that I had to get my sister and get out of the room. I felt my way over to my sister's bed, all the while watching this dark figure turn and follow my movement. I could actually feel it watching me.

The one thing that I noticed about the dark figure is that it stayed in the center of the room and did not come any closer. Again, I heard a voice say, "Don't be afraid." Again, I didn't listen.

I woke up my twin sister and told her to grab her blanket and pillow. Whispering, I told her that we had to leave the room because something was in the room that I did not like. I asked her if she could see the dark figure in our room. She said no, which scared me even more.

Holding my sister's hand, we walk around this dark figure back to my bed. I grabbed my pillow and blanket. Leading my sister I followed the wall until I reached the bedroom door. We ran to my parents' room across the hall.

I woke my mom up and told her that we needed to sleep in her room because something "bad" was in our room. She told me it was okay to sleep in their room and then added…it's just a storm and everything would be okay. There was nothing to be afraid of.

My sister and I spread out our blankets on the floor. I looked up to see where the dark figure was. It was moving again! This time it was coming toward my parents' room. I told my mom that I needed to shut the door. For some reason I told myself that this dark figure couldn't come into my parents' room if the door was shut.

I quickly ran to the door and slammed it shut, and just as quickly ran back to my blanket and pillow. I stood there waiting for something to happen, but nothing did. I must have stood there for five minutes. What was truly amazing is that I had forgotten that it was still storming outside until once again lightning lit up the room. The dark figure was gone!

During the next 14 years many things happened that I could not explain. I had strange dreams and visions and I began to hear voices in my head. I would get these feelings that I could not explain. It was like I knew something was about to happen, and then it would. I was convinced that I was evil. Haunted, even!

I made an appointment to see a well-known psychic. I told no one. The times that I had tried to communicate to my family and/or friends, I was told I had a vivid imagination. I was laughed at and made fun of. I was asked to not talk about my dreams anymore because they were scarying people. I learned to not talk about my experiences with anyone.

When I met with the psychic, I told her that I did not really want her to read my cards, but instead I wanted her to make all this evil stuff disappear. I shared the story of the dark figure that was still haunting me! She smiled at me with understanding, and on that day, my world opened up.

This beautiful, kind person helped me to understand it all. I will forever be thankful to her. I met with her several times and she helped me to understand my gift. I learned not to fear, but instead, to accept my ability. She even explained the "dark figure" in my room.

It was a visitation, a protection. It was not to be feared. Now I understood why I heard the voice tell me twice *"not to be afraid."* It wasn't telling me *not to be afraid of it*, but instead *not to be afraid of the storm*.

Wow! How simple and peaceful when you truly understand!

At the beginning of the story I wrote what's shown below, and I am ending with the same message.

"We are all on a spiritual journey…

Gift or Curse…

The choice is yours."

P.S. With Heartfelt Appreciation…Thank You, Kristen Wilkerson and Annette Matthews!

CPSIA information can be obtained at www.ICGtesting.com
Printed in the USA
LVOW041404260912

300425LV00002B/11/P

9 781452 555355